PASSAGEWAYS
AND
PROVENCE

RIVER CRUISE
COZIES
BOOK TWO

CHERYL DOUGAN

PASSAGEWAYS AND PROVENCE

A RIVER CRUISING COZY MYSTERY

CHERYL DOUGAN

DOUGAN PRESS

DOUGAN PRESS

This is the SECOND EDITION.
Previously published by Friesen Press in 2020.

Read a sample of the first chapter of the next book for free!
All you have to do is visit this link, https://tinyurl.com/cheryldougan3, enter your email address, and the free chapter will be on its way to you!

Interior Design by STOKE Publishing.

CONTENTS

CHAPTER 1
LYON
REVERSE IT ALL

Tilly swirled her wine in the sunlight. "To reverse-it-all," she declared.

"Reverse-it-all?" Adelle asked, as she raised her glass.

"I think Sis means resveratrol," Debbie translated, her eyes dancing. "It's an antioxidant found in red grapes."

Tilly rolled her eyes. "Res-whatever-it-all. Same thing only different."

The three friends burst out laughing.

It was the first hour of the first day of their river cruise from Lyon to Avignon, and Adelle was excited. As the tour host for four other women, she was thankful that the cruise line would be taking care of the details for the next eight days. Although the two extra days in Paris with the sisters had been fun, they had also been exhausting. Tilly wanted every hour to be planned and organized. She had arrived at the airport with a checklist, a very long checklist, of all the places she wanted to see in Paris. The Eiffel Tower, every museum, every art gallery. Her younger and more outgoing sister, Debbie, had her own list. She wanted to shop. And talk to everyone in each of the long lineups they endured at the busy tourist attractions. Adelle was played out. As she propped her feet up on a footstool, she looked forward to spending the rest of the afternoon relaxing before Barb and the newcomer met them at dinner.

"Too bad Teresa couldn't be here," Debbie said.

"My grandson oogled her," Tilly said, swirling her wine again. "As they say back home, she's some kind of high shot."

Oogled her? High shot? Adelle struggled not to laugh.

"Tilly," Debbie groaned, turning to her much older sister. "He googled her. Google. With a 'g.'"

Tilly rolled her eyes. "Whatever."

It had been Teresa's idea to go on a second river cruise together. What could be better than starting in Lyon, then gliding through the legendary landscapes of Provence to historic Avignon, enjoying wine tasting and French cuisine along the way? She must have had a very good reason for canceling at the last minute. Adelle wondered if Debbie or Tilly knew anything.

Adelle, a professional tour host doesn't gossip.

Adelle changed the topic to the weather, with temporary success. Debbie started talking about the other member of their group. "At least you won't have to share a cabin with Barb again."

Adelle shuddered, recalling her first impression of Barb when they met on the river cruise from Budapest to Amsterdam. It hadn't started out well.

But all is well that ends well. She smiled and sipped her wine.

Teresa's replacement in the group would be sharing a cabin with Barb this trip. Maureen, their travel agent, had assured Adelle that the newcomer was *lovely*. Adelle hoped so.

Tilly yawned and soon all three women were yawning. They had been up early to pack and catch the high-speed train from Paris to Lyon. Having just arrived on the ship, they were getting drowsy as they enjoyed a glass of wine.

"Time for my nap," Tilly announced.

Debbie jumped up. She pulled Adelle's footstool out from under her feet. "Let's go," she announced. "You promised to join me for the welcome walk!"

A martyr would have followed Debbie without hesitation. Adelle hesitated. After listening to Tilly go on and on about Marie Antoinette for the last two days, Adelle knew she was no martyr.

"You go ahead. I'll meet you in a few minutes." Maybe she could be lovely and eat her cake, too. *Good one, Adelle.* Debbie went ahead without her.

Adelle reached the paved path at the bottom of the ramp. Just as she had hoped, there was Debbie. Bouncing from foot to foot, hands flapping, talking and laughing in the middle of a dozen assembled passengers. Tilly was right, behavior was consistent and therefore predictable. Debbie always liked to be in the spotlight. Adelle grinned. Now she could enjoy a quiet stroll by herself.

Adelle noticed a woman standing off to the side of the group. She looked beat. Her white, shoulder length hair was tousled, and her black sweater was bunching up over the waist of her baggy black slacks. The signs of jet lag were unmistakable. Adelle felt sorry for her; she was obviously on her own.

"A beautiful afternoon to go for a walk," Adelle said. Talking about the weather was almost always a surefire icebreaker.

The woman continued to stare at her feet.

Adelle tried again. "Hi, I'm Adelle."

Flinching, the woman looked up, rolled her shoulders and stretched her neck from side to side. "Sorry, I think my manners have gone to sleep. I'm Evelyn." She ran her fingers through her hair and tugged on her sweater. "Nice to meet you."

On the walk into Old Lyon, Adelle learned that Evelyn had just arrived from the airport after having traveled all night.

"Annie said I should go for a walk to reset my body clock."

"Who is Annie?"

"My daughter. She's back in our cabin, catching up on a few things."

Adelle and Evelyn followed the small group over the bridge, and found themselves on the cobblestones of Vieux Lyon, the old section of Lyon. They marveled at the rows of outdoor cafés and bistros, the ancient fountain, and people bustling through the old square in every direction. The ship's program director had told them that a local guide would give them a more in-depth tour the next morning. For now, they would have an hour to look around before she led them back to the ship.

"Do you smell coffee?" Evelyn asked, sniffing the air, eyes closed.

Adelle inhaled the intense, bold scent of roasting beans wafting across the square. She smiled. "Follow me."

The two new friends discovered that in addition to coffee, they shared a love of French pastries, especially the rich chocolate croissants.

"Do I have chocolate on my face?" asked Evelyn.

"No," Adelle replied. "Do I?" She knew she could trust Evelyn to tell the truth. Unlike her husband, Wes, who always replied "no" without even looking. She smiled as she thought of Wes, remembering their embrace when he dropped her off at the airport. He was eager to help his friend harvest the wheat crop, as it gave him a break from his farm accounting practice. Adelle was also looking for a break from the boredom of retirement. She liked living on the Prairies, but cruising in Europe with her girlfriends was definitely her happy place.

Evelyn mentioned that this was her first cruise. She asked Adelle how it would work.

"There will be a local guide at each port who will

lead us on a walking tour, usually in the mornings. Then we have free time in the afternoons."

"This trip has already exceeded my wildest expectations," Evelyn gushed, gazing over the square. "My husband and I always put traveling off until he retired but …" She stared down at her hands, her chin trembling before she looked back up. "He passed away six months to the day after his retirement."

"I'm so sorry," Adelle said softly. Her heart ached for her new friend.

Evelyn stirred her coffee, lips quivering. Looking around, she smiled weakly then sat up a little straighter. "But that was then, and this is now."

Adelle admired Evelyn's courageous and positive attitude. She tried to think of an appropriate response, but nothing came to mind.

"I hope the food on board is as tasty as these croissants," Evelyn said as she gathered up the last of the crumbs and popped them in her mouth.

"The chefs are fantastic," Adelle said, relieved by the change of topic. "They will treat us to regional dishes using local produce." She could taste the meals already. "The ship even has its own herb garden on the top deck."

"And the pastries?"

"To die for."

Adelle looked away. *Why did I say die? Will I ever stop and think before I blurt out the wrong thing?* She didn't know what to say. They had already talked about the weather.

Evelyn cleared her throat. "Adelle? Can I ask you something?"

Evelyn was smiling. Maybe Adelle hadn't hurt her feelings after all.

"Do you want to split another chocolate croissant with me?" Evelyn asked with a smirk.

At that moment, Adelle knew she had found a new best friend forever.

As Evelyn divided the third croissant in half, she asked Adelle if she was on the cruise by herself.

"I'm traveling with four other women," Adelle replied. First, she briefly described Debbie and her older sister Tilly. They lived far apart and enjoyed traveling together each year to keep up their relationship.

"And the other two women?" Evelyn asked.

"One is new to our group." Adelle hadn't met her yet. She hoped she would fit in. "The other woman is half our age, and twice as energetic." She licked the last of the heavenly chocolate from her lips. "Believe it or not, on our first trip together, she worked almost the whole time."

"Sounds like my Annie," Evelyn said, licking her fork clean. "What's with this generation? So busy all the time."

"They never have time to sit down to have a conversation. They're constantly distracted by their phones." Sometimes Adelle wished cell phones had never been invented. She missed the personal connection with people. Sitting down and talking, one-on-one. *Like now.*

"I'm always asking Annie to put her phone down,

but there's no point. She twitches when it vibrates. I know I've lost her full attention when she can't stand it anymore and sneaks a glance at her screen." Evelyn frowned. "Sometimes I feel like her phone is coming between us."

Adelle knew the feeling. The technology revolution was supposed to be advancing civilization, but she wondered if it had caused people to be *less* civil. She remembered a conversation with her niece, who had argued that texting and social media created the ability to connect with more people. Adelle had argued that quantity was different than quality. Face-to-face conversations were so much better. It was one of the things she liked about traveling, the ability to meet and get to know other people better.

"Maybe you could introduce the young woman to Annie," Evelyn chuckled. "They could text each other."

Adelle wondered if that would be a good idea. On the one hand, Barb would probably appreciate being with people more her own age. Tilly was old enough to be her grandmother!

You're no spring chicken either, Adelle.

On the other hand, Barb could be prickly sometimes.

"When I first met her, she seemed self-centered, arrogant, and aloof." Adelle winced at the memory. "She even expected me to fetch her coffee in the morning. I really started to resent her but then …" Adelle felt a tap on her shoulder and turned around.

"Sorry to interrupt your conversation," Debbie said,

one eyebrow raised. "The cruise director sent me over to tell you it's time to head back to the ship."

Adelle wished she could erase what had just happened. To "reverse-it-all." But she couldn't. She'd been busted. Gossiping.

———

Adelle looked around the ship's restaurant as she and the sisters waited for Barb and the newcomer to join them for dinner. The room was large with floor-to-ceiling windows and a panoramic view of the Rhône River.

Adelle was determined to be a better tour host on this trip. She was upset with herself that Debbie had overheard her gossiping that afternoon with Evelyn. Adelle knew she had made a lot of mistakes on their first trip together. This time she would be more professional. *You can do this,* she reminded herself.

Debbie was the first to see Barb enter the restaurant. "You made it!" she exclaimed, jumping up to greet her.

"I'm beat," Barb said as she plopped down in the chair facing the entrance. "I haven't taken a break for eleven hours—" she glanced at her phone, "—and forty-seven minutes."

Tilly snorted. "I see you're still connected to that thing. It's like it's another limb."

Barb grinned. "Missed you too, Tilly."

Adelle laughed along with her friends. She wished

she could be like Tilly. Unlike Adelle, she wasn't at all intimidated by Barb.

"Who's your new cabinmate?" Debbie asked. She looked over Adelle's shoulder at the entrance. "Where is she?"

The corners of Barb's lips turned up slightly. "It's a good thing my aunt Maureen runs a travel agency. She found the perfect last-minute replacement."

Debbie leaned forward at the same as Tilly. "Who?" they asked in unison.

Adelle was also curious. Who could possibly be perfect in Barb's eyes? *Probably someone younger, and more with the times.*

Barb grinned. "Here she comes now."

Adelle turned.

Evelyn?

"Everyone, this is my mother. Evelyn."

Mother?

Flustered, Adelle knocked her wine glass over. Grabbing her napkin to dab at the spreading pink stain, she knocked her water glass over. As she tried to catch it, she felt her chair starting to tilt. She held her breath. She knew she was going down.

Bang!

The restaurant went silent. Everyone was staring at Adelle. All she could hear was her heart thumping in her chest. As she scrambled to stand up, she suddenly remembered how the sisters had recovered at the Budapest spa during the previous cruise. She winked at her girlfriends, turned to face the other passengers, and bent at the waist in an elaborate curtsy. Debbie, Tilly, and Barb burst out laughing and clapping. Soon all the passengers were joining in the applause before turning back to their own tables.

"Adelle, are you okay?" Evelyn asked as she picked up Adelle's chair, and put it back in place.

"I thought your daughter's name was Annie," Adelle spluttered.

"Mother, I asked you not call me that any more. It's so unprofessional."

"Sorry." Evelyn turned back to Adelle. "Annie … I mean Bar-ba-ra" she said, slowly enunciating each syllable, "is named after Barbara Ann Scott, the world champion figure skater."

"Bar-ba-ra Ann," Tilly said, mimicking Evelyn's pronunciation. "Nice."

"So?" Barb shot back at Tilly. "Ma-till-da."

Debbie rolled her eyes and laughed.

"Barbara seemed such a big name for such a tiny baby," Evelyn continued. "And Barbie was a doll's name. But trust me, she was no doll. She cried constantly for the first few months. It was a vicious cycle. We couldn't decide if she was hungry, or if she was full and colicky, or if her diaper needed changing, or …"

Barb groaned. "Mother, I think they get the picture." She moved aside to let their server attend to the mess on their table.

"We nicknamed her Annie, and it stuck. Until she went away to college, and came back as Bar-ba-ra."

Adelle was relieved when their meal was served. She was still reeling from the shock that Annie, *Bar-ba-ra*, *Barb*, was lovely Evelyn's daughter.

Everyone raved about the delicious dinner.

"Way better than Paris," Debbie exclaimed.

"I've never been to Paris," Evelyn confessed. "What did you like the best?"

"The shopping," Debbie replied. "Especially on the Champs-Élysées."

"Which was by the Arc de Triomphe," Tilly interjected before Debbie could get going on her favorite topic. "It's surrounded by a traffic circle."

"Some call it a roundabout," Debbie said, orbiting her left hand with her right hand.

"Whatever," Tilly said, moving her wine glass out of harm's way. Her eyes sparkled. "Twelve lanes go around the arch."

"There we were, at the top of the arch, with breathtaking views of Paris," Debbie cut in, "and my sister was studying the traffic."

Adelle chuckled. Tilly could have spent hours there.

"You don't see that back home," Tilly huffed. "The arch is at least fifteen stories high, so we had a bird's-eye view. The cars and trucks and buses and motorcycles already in the circle have to yield to the vehicles entering the circle."

"Picture this," Debbie said, making space around her dinner plate. "This is the arch. Imagine twelve lanes circling it." The women scrambled to move all the glasses out of the way as Debbie waved her hands around the plate. "Now picture the drivers yielding to another four lanes coming into the circle." Debbie demonstrated the chaos using her cutlery. "Four lanes trying to enter, while the vehicles already in the circle were maneuvering to exit." She threw her hands up in the air. "From twelve approaching avenues!"

"Horns blaring," Tilly added. "Vehicles going every which way." She folded her hands on her lap and grinned. "It was quite the show. I'll never forget it."

Debbie agreed. "I'll show you our video later."

Of course, you will, thought Adelle. Debbie was always taking photos and videos to post on her social media accounts. While she fiddled with her cell phone, she was missing so much. Adelle preferred to file the experiences away in her memory. Although the posts were helpful reminders; her memory wasn't what it used to be.

That's when Adelle remembered what she had said about Barb that afternoon. To her mother, no less! *But it was the truth.* Barb was arrogant, especially when she was talking about her technological and analytical skills. Adelle was so intimidated by her. She wanted to understand what she was saying, but it was like a foreign language. Adelle usually tuned her out.

As their friendly server cleared their plates away, Debbie described their first dinner in Paris, near the Eiffel Tower.

"First, Sis insisted on ordering everything in French." Debbie rolled her eyes and chuckled. "Even though the waiter answered her first question in English."

Tilly crossed her arms. "Learning and using another language is good for the brain. I did just fine."

"Until you tried to order the steak tartare well-done," Debbie said.

Barb smirked. "Well-done, raw ground meat? Good one, Tilly."

"The story gets better," Debbie continued. "Tilly ordered 'Vicky's sauce.' Then she complained to our waiter that it was cold."

"Vicky's sauce?" Evelyn asked.

"Vichyssoise," explained Debbie. "Chilled potato and leek soup."

"What's wrong with good old-fashioned meat and potatoes?" Tilly protested. "Imagine serving raw meat and cold soup on the farm. Unheard of."

The sisters and Evelyn launched into an animated conversation about French cooking. And boutique shopping. And crafts. Adelle sat back and sipped her wine. *Evelyn is lovely. She fits in so well.* Then a niggling thought crept into Adelle's brain. Evelyn hadn't made eye contact with her since before dinner was served.

Why is Evelyn ignoring me? Adelle wondered.

You trashed her daughter. To her face.

Adelle suddenly remembered that she hadn't finished telling Evelyn the rest of the story about Barb on their first trip. No wonder she wouldn't look at her.

Before Adelle could figure out what to do next, dinner was over.

"What are you working on, Barb?" Tilly asked, pushing away from the table.

"I could tell you," Barb replied, "but then I would have to throw you overboard."

Everyone laughed. Except Adelle. *Why does Barb always have to be so secretive?*

As Barb and the sisters left the table, Adelle knew she had to finish her conversation with Evelyn or she would be wide-awake all night, worrying.

"Evelyn, do you have a minute?"

Evelyn smiled and sat back down.

"I'm so sorry what I said about Barb!" Adelle blurted. "I didn't know you were her mother! I didn't get the chance to tell you the rest of the story—"

Evelyn held up her hand, eyes twinkling. "Before you apologize any further, you need to know something." Evelyn grinned. "I agree with what you said."

"You do?"

"I couldn't look at you during dinner. If I did, I would have burst out laughing. I know my daughter can appear self-centered and arrogant. Don't get me wrong. I love her to the moon and back, but she's a little socially awkward."

There's an understatement.

"After watching her interactions at dinner, I can see where you're coming from." Evelyn pointed at Adelle. "You've got icing on your chin."

"I didn't get a chance to finish my story earlier," Adelle said, wiping the icing away. "When we first met, Barb seemed … difficult. However, as I got to know her

15

better I realized she was … intelligent, and … serious about her work."

Evelyn laughed. "She takes after her father. He was also smart and driven by his career. He was a judge."

Maybe that's why I always feel like she is judging me, Adelle thought. Something else bothered her. "Do you understand what Barb does in her job?"

"Not really," Evelyn confessed. "When I ask her about it, she says—"

"'… you wouldn't understand'," Adelle chimed in.

They burst out laughing at Barb's standard answer to every question.

Adelle shook her head. "I didn't expect Barb's cabinmate to be her mother. I should have guessed that when she told us you were the perfect replacement."

"She said that about me?" Evelyn glowed. "Thanks for sharing that."

"You're welcome."

There, you've officially welcomed the newcomer. Adelle tried not to grin. *Enough wine for you. Time to go to bed.*

As they left the restaurant, Adelle linked arms with Evelyn. "I'm surprised you didn't guess who Debbie and I were yesterday. Didn't Barb tell you about traveling with us on our first cruise?"

Evelyn glanced quickly at Adelle, then looked away. "As you've probably observed, she's very private and confidential about her work."

It's so frustrating!

"When she arrived home from Europe, all she said

was that she met …" Evelyn's voice trailed off, and her neck flushed deep red.

"Yes?" Adelle prompted.

Evelyn turned to Adelle, the corners of her mouth twitching. "She said she met some old geezers."

"Old geezers?" Adelle spluttered. *The nerve! After all we did for her!*

Evelyn was obviously trying not to laugh. "Don't be offended, Adelle. She thinks everyone older than forty is *ancient*. Including her mother."

Adelle thought about her own children. When they were young, she and Wes were smart. Between the teenage years and young adulthood, she and Wes were anything *but* smart. Now that Adelle and Wes were grandparents, they were simply old. *Ancient.*

Evelyn chuckled. "I should have twigged when you told me that your cabinmate expected you to bring her coffee each morning."

"One-third regular, two-thirds decaf, and lots of hot milk," Adelle said.

Good memory … for an old geezer.

———

"It's beautiful," Evelyn whispered as they wandered down the aisle of the Basilica of Notre-Dame de Fourvière on the morning tour of Lyon.

Adelle agreed. From the stained-glass windows, to the ornate hanging lights, to the millions of tiny inlaid mosaic tiles, the church was breathtaking. She tried not to tip over backwards as she admired the beautiful ceiling paintings.

Once outside, they took in the panoramic view of the red-tiled roofs of Old Lyon with the Alps in the background.

"Did you hear the guide when he said Lyon was founded by the Romans in 43 BC?" Evelyn asked excitedly. "People have lived here over two thousand years!"

Adelle was amused by Evelyn's child-like enthusiasm for everything. The omelet at breakfast was "the best" she had ever tasted, and their motor coach was "the most modern bus" she had ever traveled in. Adelle looked forward to learning more about Lyon through the eyes of her new friend.

Barb had announced at breakfast that she wasn't going on the excursion. She had work to do. *Maybe you'll learn what her daughter is working on, too.*

The friends caught up to the local guide as he was pointing at the towers on each corner of the basilica. "When you return to Old Lyon, be sure to look back up at this spot. You'll see why the locals call the basilica the 'upside-down elephant.'"

The young man directed their attention down the hill. "If you like to shop, you will find the Presqu'ile shopping district there," he advised, pointing at the finger of land between the Rhône and Saône rivers below.

"We know where Debbie will take you shopping this afternoon," Adelle whispered to Evelyn, as they continued to walk behind their guide to the nearby remains of two Gallo-Roman amphitheaters.

Better her than me, thought Adelle, grateful that Evelyn was eager to go with Debbie. In Adelle's mind, anything was better than shopping. She supposed it had all started when she was young. It wasn't any fun when your family was poor. When she was older, she didn't lack funds, she lacked confidence. She always felt at the mercy of pushy shop clerks. When Adelle retired, she still had expensive outfits in her closet that had never been worn. Some still had the price tags on. One suit was particularly atrocious. It had wide black and yellow stripes. *No wonder you never wore it, you looked like a bumblebee.*

The smaller Roman theater, called the Odeon, had been built in the second century AD and was used for poetry and music recitals. The larger amphitheater had been built under the reign of Emperor Augustus. Adelle was surprised that it was still being used for performances, even though it was "ancient," built around 15 BC.

Now that's *ancient,* thought Adelle. She was still rankled by Barb's comments.

Let it go, Adelle. Let it go.

After boarding their motor coach, the group continued their tour past the magnificent Cathédrale Saint-Jean-Baptiste into one of the largest old quarters in Europe. When Lyon's silk industry was thriving, from the fifteenth century to the seventeenth century, rich merchant families had settled there, building extravagant Renaissance homes.

They stopped at the famous Painted Houses. In the seventies, a group of Lyon students had been sitting around, discussing the art world. They decided that murals could help bring art to everyday people. The paintings could also help citizens better trace their history and rediscover their identity. The students' discussion coincided with a civic movement to brighten up Lyon by rejuvenating the public squares and historic buildings. An idea was born. The muralists found themselves in the right place at the right time.

Adelle and Evelyn stared up at the mural known as La Fresque des Lyonnais, the mural of the people of Lyon. It covered two sides of a large windowless building on a corner alongside the Saône River. It had been created using the trompe l'oeil painting technique, which translated to "deceiving the eye." At first glance, Adelle was definitely deceived. She thought she saw a very busy building, with people standing on balconies and people walking by the street-level shops.

"It's the biggest painting I've ever seen," Evelyn cried.

Their guide pointed out twenty-four historical persons and six contemporary figures. They were all so lifelike. Adelle resisted the urge to wave to Roman Emperor Claudius, whose image seemed to be looking down at her from the third level.

"Look, there's Paul Bocuse!" Evelyn exclaimed,

pointing at an image of a chef standing in the doorway of the painted street-level café.

"Who is Paul Bocuse?" Adelle asked.

Evelyn turned to her, eyebrows raised. "You don't know who Paul Bocuse is?"

"A French celebrity?"

"One of the most famous chefs in the world," exclaimed Evelyn. "I thought everyone knew who Paul Bocuse is."

"I don't cook," Adelle admitted. "My husband is the cook in our family." From the age of ten, she had to cook for her family, but she had gladly given it up when she married Wes. He liked cooking. Since he had a home office, he said it gave him a break from his work. Adelle had always thought she would take up cooking again when she retired. That lasted for less than a week. Thankfully, Wes took over the kitchen again. She didn't miss cooking at all.

Adelle wondered how the harvest was going. Because of the time difference, she and Wes had agreed to leave short texts for each other every few days. In his last text, he was worried about the weather forecast. Time is money, he was fond of saying.

The traboules nearby were fascinating. They were Renaissance-era passageways that gave the city's silk workers direct access to the riverbank, offering shelter from the elements. Approximately forty passageways were still accessible to the public. Their entranceways were marked by a small identifying seal. Walking single file, the group silently followed their guide through old buildings, small courtyards, and up then down staircases.

"Too bad Barb didn't come," Evelyn said afterward. "She has always been interested in mazes and puzzles. She would have loved the traboules."

Adelle had an idea. Their ship was docked nearby. If Barb could spare an hour, Adelle could walk with her back to the passageways after lunch. Better yet, maybe Tilly would like to do that. Then Adelle could indulge in her favorite activity, meeting other people on the cruise. Wes was always teasing her about her interest in other people and their paths. "Paffs" he would say, mimicking her "happy birfday" pronunciation. It was strange. Path and birthday were the only two words she unconsciously mispronounced. Like her granddaughter, she realized. Adelle turned and looked up at the basilica, smiling at the "ephelant."

"In 1998, ten percent of Lyon was listed as an UNESCO World Heritage site," their guide proudly stated.

"Teresa would have loved this trip," Adelle whispered to Evelyn. She could almost hear Teresa describing each architectural feature of the well-preserved old neighborhood. *In great detail.*

Evelyn stopped walking. She turned to Adelle. "Who's Teresa?"

"She's the woman who was supposed to stay with Barb, but she had to cancel," Adelle replied. "Why do you ask?"

Evelyn looked at her feet, and tugged her sweater down.

"Barb was talking quietly to Teresa on the phone late last night. She thought I was sleeping. When I asked her about it this morning, all she would say was that Teresa needed some help finding something."

"I wonder what she's looking for?" Adelle prompted.

Evelyn was silent.

"I'll ask her at lunch," Adelle said.

Evelyn flinched. "Please don't. I promised Barb I wouldn't say anything." She moaned. "I shouldn't have told you."

"Don't worry, Evelyn. I promise I won't let on I know about Teresa." Adelle grinned and winked. "I can't swim."

Evelyn burst out laughing. "Thanks! I don't swim either!"

As they continued their tour, Adelle thought about gregarious Teresa and introverted Barb, and how they had bonded on the first river cruise. By the time their cruise had ended in Amsterdam, the two were often huddled together over Barb's laptop. As Tilly had wryly observed, they could talk about spreadsheets and analytics until the cows came home.

Better Teresa than me, thought Adelle. She didn't have the foggiest idea what Barb was talking about half the time anyway. Maybe Teresa was getting Barb to do research for her company. But why was Barb always so secretive? And why hadn't Barb told her mom anything about the girls, or what had happened on their last trip?

Adelle stumbled on the cobblestones. *Pick up your feet, you old geezer.*

After lunch Adelle went up to the deck. She was looking forward to meeting the other passengers while Debbie and Evelyn were shopping and Tilly and Barb were exploring the passageways. She snatched a sheet of paper fluttering by before it blew overboard. Looking around, she saw an elderly woman sitting at a table by the opposite railing, trying to prevent more papers from blowing away.

"Did you lose this?" Adelle asked the plump woman with the curly white hair and dark sunglasses. There was something about her that reminded Adelle of Mrs. Santa Claus.

The woman's name was Mickey, and she thanked Adelle profusely and invited her to sit and visit. She was a retired mathematics teacher who described herself as sweet sixteen, plus five, plus four times fifteen.

"Eighty-one!" blurted Adelle, always the people-pleaser, especially when teachers were concerned. Mickey was impressed and asked Adelle if she had always been good with numbers. Their conversation led to Adelle's career.

"I worked in the hero to bum business," Adelle said.

Mickey's forehead wrinkled above her sunglasses.

"Financial services," explained Adelle. "When markets went up I was a hero. When markets went down I felt like a bum."

Mickey laughed. "You can't control the markets, any more than the ship's captain can control the weather."

After decades as an investment advisor, Adelle had finally come to the same conclusion. She had eventually gravitated to the non-financial side of retirement planning, turning the day-to-day portfolio management over to her two capable partners. That left her free to talk to her clients about their retirement lifestyle goals.

"People were very concerned about the amount of money they were saving," Adelle said, "but they had no idea what they were saving it for." She chuckled.

"What's so funny?" Mickey asked.

"Now that I'm retired, I understand where my clients were coming from," Adelle said. "Here I am. Retired. Without a retirement plan."

Mickey laughed. "Like a plumber with leaky taps." She smoothed the retrieved paper on the top of her pile. "Or a teacher without students."

Adelle noticed a big heart, a stick man, a cloud, and a question mark, all shakily drawn in red.

Mickey explained that she had promised to give a presentation to her seniors' group. "This is my cheat sheet," she said. "It reminds me what to include in case I get sidetracked." She held up a red crayon. "This reminds me not to take myself too seriously. To color outside the lines and have fun."

"Like a toddler with no fear," Adelle said.

"Right!" replied Mickey. "I want to share how we need to be accountable for our own lives. The things we want don't just magically happen, we need to take action."

Mickey pointed at the big heart. "For example, relationships. If we want to have a friend, we have to be a friend."

Simple enough.

"What does the cloud represent?" asked Adelle, curious.

"The mind," replied Mickey. "We need mental exercise as much as physical exercise."

While Mickey talked about the importance of exercising the brain, Adelle made a mental note to connect Mickey and Tilly.

"Let me guess," Adelle said, after bringing them each a coffee. "The stick man stands for our body."

"A-plus," exclaimed Mickey, thumb up. "I like to talk about the three e's: *exercising*, *eating* properly, and getting *enough* sleep." She picked up the red crayon, and drew a large "E" beside the stick man. "To jog my memory," she said, smiling.

The women were startled by a loud high-pitched whining noise alongside the ship.

"What is that?" Mickey asked, jerking her head toward the river.

Adelle stood up and looked over the side of the railing.

"A Jet Ski," Adelle replied. She described the young

male driver executing tight figure eights beside the docked ship.

Mickey giggled.

"Have you ever driven a Jet Ski?" Adelle asked, sitting back down.

"Not yet!" cried Mickey, grinning widely.

Not yet? Adelle laughed, picturing her new friend piloting a Jet Ski.

The breeze ruffled Mickey's papers.

"What does the question mark stand for?" Adelle asked, glancing back down at the papers.

"Soul, spirit, purpose, whatever works for you," Mickey replied. She chuckled. "One of my friends has started reading her Bible again. She told me she was cramming for finals."

Good one.

"Others think about their purpose in life. Or, as they say here in France, their 'raison d'être,' their reason for existing."

Existing. Adelle realized that her life had come down to simply *existing.* But she didn't want to simply exist, she wanted to be fully alive! Before retirement she had a purpose in her life, a career that made her feel needed and appreciated. Her day planner was always full—every hour of her day was booked solid. Client appointments, board meetings, volunteer events. A reason to get up each morning, excited to meet whatever the day had in store. Adelle sighed. She hadn't felt that way for a long time.

"There you are, Adelle!"

Adelle saw Debbie and Evelyn walking over to their table. As Debbie introduced herself to Mickey, Evelyn pulled Adelle off to the side.

"I overheard Barb talking to Teresa on her cell phone again," Evelyn whispered.

Adelle wondered if Tilly had already taught Evelyn to rubberneck.

"A significant amount of money is missing," Evelyn said. "Barb is trying to find it."

Adelle was shocked. That's why Teresa hadn't come.

She needs help.

Evelyn must have read her mind. "Adelle, you promised not to say anything to Barb."

Adelle was torn. She wanted to help, but she didn't want to break her promise to Evelyn.

How can I help Barb help Teresa without Barb knowing? I can't involve Debbie because she will tell Tilly. Adelle knew it was impossible for Tilly to keep a secret. Was there another way? She was tempted to not try. It would be easier to stay in her own lane.

Adelle noticed Mickey holding her papers down as Debbie's hands flew in every direction while she was talking.

Mickey wouldn't give up, and neither will I. Not yet!

CHAPTER 2
BEAUJOLAIS
IT MAKES NO NEVER MIND

Arriving at the winery, Adelle was delighted that there were still some grape bunches on the vine, even though the harvest was done. The Gamay grapes were different than Adelle had expected. She was surprised how small they were. A bunch fit into the palm of her hand with each deep purple grape being the size of the end of her finger. She sampled one, expecting a bitter taste.

"These are the sweetest grapes I've ever tasted," Evelyn exclaimed beside her.

Adelle chuckled at Evelyn's enthusiasm. She wished she had sat with Evelyn on the motor coach trip from the ship in Lyon to the beautiful Beaujolais region. But she had arranged to ride with Tilly because she had wanted to find out how she and Barb got along so well. It seemed like a simple math equation. If Tilly liked Barb and they got along, and if Adelle liked Tilly and they got along, then she should be able to get along with Barb, too. Then she could figure out how to help Teresa.

On the drive to the winery, Tilly seemed content to sit quietly and knit.

"What are you knitting, Tilly?"

"Comfort dolls," Tilly replied, needles flying. She was making knitted dolls to donate to children in need. Adelle imagined the cuddly doll nestling in the crook of a small child's arm.

"I've got extra needles," Tilly said, reaching into her shoulder bag. "I'll show you how."

Adelle stifled a groan. Handiwork was not her forte. As Tilly soon found out.

"You're all thumbs," snorted an exasperated Tilly, taking back the needles and tangled yarn. "Just like Barb with that phone of hers."

This is your chance, Adelle.

"How was your afternoon with Barb yesterday?" she asked. She was pleased that Barb had agreed to take an hour after lunch to explore the covered passageways with Tilly. "Did she tell you what she was working on?"

Way to blurt, Adelle. So much for patience.

"We don't spend our time yakking like the rest of you," Tilly replied, frowning as she tried to untangle the yarn. Then she sat up, looking smug. "We had a contest to see who could find the most traboules. Let's just say she won't be bringing that up."

Adelle smiled, imagining them darting around the passageways. She knew how competitive Barb was. And Tilly.

"You won, and you're still friends?" Adelle asked, trying to keep her voice light.

"Of course," Tilly replied, shoving the knot of yarn into her bag. "Why wouldn't we be? I beat her fair and square."

Maybe they have similar interests.

As the motor coach turned onto the winery's driveway, Tilly was once again exasperated. "Adelle, you don't shop, you don't cook, you don't do crafts, you don't garden." She shook her head. "What, pray tell, do you do all day?"

Good question, Adelle thought to herself. After retirement, it seemed like she was busier than when she was working. How had she ever managed to work full time, take courses, attend endless committee meetings, raise a family, go to the grandchildren's events, and on and on?

Now you're too busy doing nothing to have time to do anything else.

When they arrived at the winery, Adelle was grateful to join Evelyn strolling between rows of ripe, purple grapes.

"Adelle and Evelyn, here you are," exclaimed Debbie, dragging Tilly behind her. "Can one of you video Tilly and me picking these tasty grapes?" Tilly grimaced. She hated getting her photo taken, and disliked videos even more. Then she broke into a grin.

Who is Tilly smiling at?

"Bonjour Jean-Luc," Tilly sang.

Adelle turned to see their tour guide strolling up to their group. Jean-Luc was very tall, with twinkling eyes and the most striking bushy beard Adelle had ever seen.

It was streaked with auburn and gray, and reached to the middle of his chest. His clothes were even more unique. He wore a black linen square-collared jacket over a black shirt, with black-and-white polka-dot pants, rolled up short above his bare ankles, and gigantic black-and-white polka-dot sneakers. He was possibly the most charming young man Adelle had ever met. No wonder Tilly was smiling!

Jean-Luc advised that it was their turn to go down into the cellar for their wine tasting.

As they followed Jean-Luc, Adelle chuckled when Debbie teased her sister about their guide.

"I'm old," Tilly replied sarcastically, "but I'm not dead."

Although Tilly was probably the most fit person in the group, she happily gave Jean-Luc her hand as he led her down the steep stairs into the cool, softly lit cellar. The walls were lined with massive wine barrels. Chairs had been placed in front of the barrels beside tables containing a variety of cheeses and crackers to accompany their wine.

"Did you notice all the vineyards on the way here?" Debbie asked as she sat down beside Adelle. "Until today, I didn't know that it was the Romans who established winemaking in the Beaujolais region." She chuckled. "Julius Caesar should have said, 'I came, I conquered, I planted grapes.'"

Jean-Luc began his presentation, demonstrating how to properly taste wine.

"First, you have to give it your full attention," he

advised, filling his glass one-third full. He raised his glass and looked at his wine appreciatively. Tilly was looking at Jean-Luc with the same expression. Adelle tried not to laugh.

He tipped the glass from side to side, checking for clarity.

"Swirl the wine in your glass," he said. "That will let more oxygen in, and the aroma out." Sniffing deeply, he closed his eyes and smiled. "You can sip it, or you can take a mouthful and swirl it around in your mouth like a mouthwash."

"Mouthwash?" Debbie whispered. "I hope Sis doesn't gargle!"

"You should detect sweetness on the tip of your tongue," Jean-Luc continued. "If there is any bitterness, it will be at the back of your tongue."

Evelyn was very interested in the wine tasting, and asked lots of questions. It was obvious to Adelle that she was an experienced hostess.

Another thing you don't do.

Just the thought of entertaining had always tied Adelle up in knots. Was the house clean enough? Were the forks and spoons in the right place? Was the menu interesting? Would anyone get food poisoning?

Food poisoning, Adelle?

She could hear Wes teasing her that she worried too much. "You need to relax more," he always teased.

As if saying "relax" ever helped anyone relax!

Adelle tried to focus on the wine's characteristics. If she could remember them, she could bluff her way through their next social event. *It's like your napkin trick*, she thought. Whenever she was dining with someone new, she showed them how to fold a napkin properly in their lap, sharing that she had learned the technique from an etiquette class. People always assumed she knew proper table etiquette. Adelle grinned. She could use her hands to scoop food from her plate, and they would *still* think that was proper.

"This is a light-bodied wine, with high acidity and low tannins," Jean-Luc commented, swirling his glass appreciatively. "Note the red berry flavors, including raspberry, red cherry, red currant, and cranberries."

Swirling another glass of red wine, he compared it to "Old World Pinot Noir, with mushroom, forest floor, and smoky notes."

Forest floor? Adelle deleted that phrase from her memory.

Answering another question from Evelyn, Jean-Luc suggested pairing the first red wine with roasted white meats like chicken, turkey, and pork, as well as light salads. He thought the second red wine would go well with mushroom dishes and creamy risottos. Adelle was already confused. *Which wine was which?*

"What about Beaujolais Nouveau?" asked Evelyn.

Jean-Luc explained that the Nouveau wine was meant to be enjoyed within six months of its release, unlike the wine aging for years in a cellar. Otherwise the fresh fruit flavors would have faded away.

Like you, Adelle. Fading away with nothing to offer anymore.

Adelle winced as Debbie elbowed her in the ribs.

"Look at that old fool," Debbie said, pointing at her sister. "She's flirting with Jean-Luc."

Adelle strained to hear Tilly.

"Wine gets better with age, Jean-Luc."

Did Tilly just wink at him?

As Debbie rolled her eyes and chuckled, Adelle straightened her shoulders. Maybe Tilly had a good point.

Adelle was relieved to ride back to the ship with Debbie after Tilly had asked to switch places with her sister. Debbie assumed she was looking for quieter company.

"Evelyn seems wonderful," Debbie commented, settling in her seat. "She looks so much younger in her new colorful silk scarf. For some reason, she only packed dark clothes."

Adelle laughed inside. Not everyone liked bright neon pink as much as Debbie.

"You would have enjoyed shopping with us yester-day," Debbie said.

Smile and nod, Adelle.

"The shops are different than at home. Have you noticed that everyone says hello when they enter a store?" Debbie waved her hand. "And goodbye when they leave?"

They talked about other cultural differences, such as walking to a neighborhood cheese store for cheese, a neighborhood bread store for bread, and a neighborhood meat store for meat. At each place everyone knew each other by name. It was so different from driving to a one-stop large grocery store where everyone was anonymous.

Adelle appreciated how quickly their ship had felt like a neighborhood community, her home away from home. After the first day, the crew greeted each of the passengers by name. Adelle was struggling to return the courtesy. Not like Evelyn, who seemingly had no problem remembering the crew members' names. Yesterday morning, she had asked Pierre, their regular server, to compliment the chef on his mouthwatering croissants. This morning, the chef had appeared at their breakfast table, presenting an entire tray of warm croissants, fresh out of the oven. "Merci Henri!" Evelyn had exclaimed, clapping her hands together.

Henri? How did she do that?

"Have you found out what Barb is doing?" Debbie asked, before Adelle could ask the same question.

"No." Adelle was tempted to say more until she remembered that Debbie had caught her gossiping the first day. She decided to change the topic. "Which red wine did you like best?"

"I like all red wine," replied Debbie after a short pause. "I've always enjoyed red wine. Did you notice how passionate the winery owner was? His family has owned their business for generations, just like our family farm." Debbie talked about growing up in the country before she got married and moved to the big city.

"Sometimes I miss living on the farm," admitted Debbie. "Tilly doesn't understand how anyone could live anywhere else."

Before Adelle could stop herself, she was telling Debbie about her earlier conversation with Tilly.

"That's my sister," Debbie said, chuckling. "She's a practical prairie farm girl. If you can't bake a flapper pie, or darn a pair of socks …"

People still do that?

"… you might as well move to the city."

Debbie told Adelle that once when she was a teenager, anxious to go into town for the day, she had hurried to dig two hundred and fifty holes to plant potatoes.

"Tilly made me fill the holes in and start all over." Debbie sighed. "Apparently, my rows were crooked." She shook her finger and scowled, impersonating her sister. "'Debbie. If you don't have time to do it right the first time, when are you going to have time to fix it?'"

"Weren't you angry?" Adelle asked. She knew she would have been.

"For a while," Debbie admitted. "Until I complained to my neighbor." She laughed.

"What did your neighbor say?" Adelle asked.

"Debbie, it makes no never mind."

Good one!

"Tilly doesn't understand, but I wouldn't exchange my business for anything," Debbie said, talking about her ladies' clothing consignment store. "It feels like I'm making a difference in people's lives."

Making a difference ...

"Some of my customers can't afford new, fashionable outfits. It's so much fun helping them find something that makes them feel good about themselves."

Adelle thought back to her childhood when her wardrobe consisted entirely of hand-me-down clothes from her older cousin. To Adelle they were new, no matter how faded and patched they were. To this day, she was thrilled any time one of her friends passed on outfits. It wasn't about the lack of funds anymore. She could afford whatever she wanted. It was just the knowledge that someone had thought about her. Someone cared.

And they have great taste!

"Who brings their clothes to sell in your store?" Adelle asked.

"A variety of women," Debbie replied. "Some sell for pin money. Some are more interested in cleaning out their closets and recycling. They ask me to give the proceeds to someone who could use it." Debbie smiled. "Before I left, a customer asked if I would use the proceeds to buy small gifts to tuck in with the purchases of those women who simply needed a lift."

What a great idea.

Then Debbie told Adelle she had acquired extra space from an adjoining business. The price was too good to pass up, but she wasn't sure what to do with it.

Adelle had an idea. Perhaps the space could be

repurposed into a small gathering area with red-and-white checked tablecloths like the ones in the outdoor French cafés. Local artists could paint murals on the walls. A local bakery could provide chocolate croissants. Debbie loved the ideas, and pulled out a notebook to make some notes.

Adelle gazed at the vineyards out the motor coach window. *I don't garden, but I'm good at planting ideas,* Adelle thought. What if she could plant ideas with Evelyn to pass on to Barb? Was that being deceitful? Maybe, maybe not. But that way, she could honor her promise not to let Barb know what she knew. *Indirectness won't hurt anyone's feelings, Adelle. Not like Tilly's bluntness.* Adelle sighed. If only she had an idea.

Adelle borrowed a sheet of paper from Debbie's notebook and started to doodle, starting with a large question mark. *Nothing.* Then she drew a heart. *Nothing.* Followed by a stick man. *Still nothing.* Next, she drew a cloud.

Bingo!

CHAPTER 3
VIENNE
YOU DON'T SEE THIS BACK HOME

Adelle had outdone herself at breakfast that morning. She couldn't decide between the buttermilk pancakes or the French toast with wild blueberry sauce. Pierre had surprised her.

You didn't have *to eat both of them,* she groaned. Then she grinned. If she had to do it over again, she would still eat them both. They were delicious!

While she enjoyed her breakfast, Adelle had quietly asked Evelyn if Barb was having any success helping Teresa. "Nothing to report," was all she said. Adelle hoped she would have an opportunity to plant her idea with Evelyn during their morning tour, which was beginning in a few minutes.

"I love how we go to sleep in one port, and wake up in another," Evelyn commented as they followed their beautiful young guide on the walking tour of Vienne.

"It's a great way to travel," agreed Adelle, "unpacking once and letting someone else take care of all the details." *Especially the details!* She didn't have to worry about planning their day, where they would eat, or what they would do.

"Vienne is the door to the south of France," their guide began, standing in a beautiful public garden beside a short path made of granite blocks. Adelle was surprised to learn that the path was actually a short section of a Roman road, unearthed when the public gardens were created. It dated to the first century AD.

It was difficult for Adelle to fathom how much of the world the Romans had once controlled. At its peak, the Roman Empire included most of Europe, northern coastal Africa, the Balkans, the Mediterranean Sea, the Black Sea, most of present-day Turkey, and some parts of the Middle East. They had built the largest and long-est-lasting network of roads, primarily used to quickly transport soldiers.

Vienne had been the capital of a Celtic tribe before it was conquered and ruled by the Romans from 121 BC to 275 AD. During the Middle Ages, Vienne was part of the kingdom of Provence. It was transferred to French sovereignty in 1450.

"When were the Middle Ages?" Evelyn asked.

Adelle paid attention as the guide described the medieval period from the fifth century to the late fifteenth century. The majority of the people lived in the country and worked as farmers, usually for a local lord. Adelle grinned, imagining Tilly as a very demanding lord indeed.

Walking on, they learned that Vienne had been an

important strategic outpost for the Roman Empire. Located at the junction of the Rhône and Gère rivers, it was well situated for commerce, and had evolved into a cultural and intellectual hub.

Weaving through the narrow streets, they found themselves in the middle of a bustling outdoor market. There were hundreds of small stalls, many protected from the elements by colorful striped awnings. Adelle loved watching the locals as they went from stall to stall, baskets in hand, shopping for everything from fresh fruits and vegetables to clothing and household goods.

Wes would love buying groceries here, thought Adelle. It was another thing she didn't do. Cooks had to shop for their *own* ingredients. Her contribution was thinking up different meal ideas, acting as the sous chef, and cleaning up afterward.

Adelle was astonished when their group walked around the corner and she found herself staring up at a very large Roman temple. As Tilly was always saying, "you don't see this back home."

The temple was built around 20 BC to honor Emperor Augustus and his wife, Livia. When the Roman Empire fell, the temple was transformed into a parish church. It was used as a club for the Jacobins during the French Revolution, and was later restored to its original appearance in 1860.

The medieval Saint Maurice Cathedral, a national monument of France, was another massive building in the center of Vienne. Adelle was amazed that it had taken over four hundred years to build. The exterior was flamboyant Gothic style while the inside featured much simpler Romanesque architecture.

Adelle paid attention when she heard their guide mention the Knights Templar. She had learned a little about the wealthy Christian fighting order on her first river cruise. It was a large organization of devout Christians established in 1119, whose initial mission was to protect European travelers on pilgrimages to the Holy Land.

The cathedral was the site of the Council of Vienne when Pope Clement V, at the request of Philip of France, who was short on funds, dissolved the Knights Templar. Their leader placed a curse on both Philip and Pope Clement, before being burned at the stake. Philip was dead within four months. His three sons died soon after. Pope Clement died within six months.

The group boarded a small tourist tram that took them up the steep hill overlooking Vienne. They wound past quaint properties with walled gardens until they reached the top, where they continued their walking tour.

"Can you imagine watching a performance here?" Evelyn asked. They were looking down on a thirteen-thousand-seat Roman semicircular theater built into the side of the steep hill. It had been buried since the fourth century until archaeologists had uncovered it in 1922.

The rows of seats were facing a modern stage, used for summer jazz concerts. Behind the stage, Adelle admired Vienne. It was framed by the Rhône River, rolling green hills and blue sky. She knew she would have trouble focusing on the stage no matter what performance was taking place. Evelyn tugged at her sleeve. The guide was leading them across the street.

Thinking of performances, Adelle remembered her plan. She wanted to plant a seed with Evelyn that she could pass on to Barb.

Patience, Adelle. Wait for the right place and time.

Their guide opened the door of the small nondescript chapel across the road. After everyone was seated, the young woman opened her folder, and set a sheet of paper on the altar in front of her. She closed her eyes and took a deep breath. Then she sang the most mesmerizing version of "Ave Maria" that Adelle had ever heard.

Leaving the chapel, Adelle noticed tears flowing down Evelyn's cheeks.

"My granddaughter told me it's okay to cry," Adelle said, swiping at her own tears. "She said it's just our heart coming out our eyes." Evelyn smiled.

While they waited for the return tram, Evelyn told Adelle why she was so emotional. "Ave Maria" had been her wedding song. Adelle listened silently as Evelyn talked about her marriage. It had been a good one. Evelyn was slowly coming to terms with being a widow. The fog was beginning to lift.

"Sorry to be such a downer," Evelyn sniffled. "Please don't tell Barb about Ave Maria. I know she can appear very insensitive sometimes." She accepted a tissue. "But you would be surprised how sensitive she actually is."

Adelle promised she wouldn't say anything.

Evelyn gestured to the sky and valley below. "It's such a nice day. Look, not a cloud in the sky."

Cloud!

Adelle struggled briefly with her conscience. She debated if she should plant the seed.

No, Adelle. Wrong time, wrong place. Maybe tonight at dinner.

Adelle enjoyed the pleasant afternoon, cruising on the Rhône. As they were passing through a lock, she struck up a conversation with the woman sitting in the deck chair next to her. She and her sisters had been on a week-long hike through rural France before their husbands joined them on the river cruise. Although it had been a good bonding experience, the woman was enjoying being pampered onboard. Adelle learned that her new friend was interested in adult education.

"Have you heard of MOOCs?" she asked. MOOCs were free online courses available to anyone with a computer and internet connection. The courses were flexible, and students could learn at their own pace. Adelle promised herself she would research them when she got back home. The local tour guides were like the archaeologists they talked about, Adelle realized. They had uncovered Adelle's long-buried curiosity.

Adelle studied the dinner menu. Finally, she decided on the filet mignon de porc noir du Pèrigord.

Pierre explained that the accompanying tarbais beans were grown locally, with sweet, milky flesh, and thin skin.

"Like you," Tilly said, teasing her sister.

Evelyn explained to Adelle that the "piquillo pepper coulis with vanilla cream" was a pepper sauce.

Adelle envied Barb. It took her less than a minute to decide before she tapped away on her phone again.

"A burger?" Tilly asked Barb. "You can eat that at home."

Barb set her phone down and read from her menu. "Burger with oyster mushrooms, arugula, and confit tomato pesto."

Mushrooms.

Adelle changed her order. At least she would know which red wine to order!

"Make sure to save room for chocolate later," Debbie advised Tilly when she ordered the vanilla-poached scallops, lobster and shrimp bisque, and potato gnocchi. The sisters laughed heartily.

"What's so funny?" Adelle asked.

"I forgot," replied Debbie. "You and Evelyn were in a different group this morning. When our group stopped in the Vienne market, Tilly wanted to buy truffles. Our guide kept pointing at one of the stalls across the square, and Sis kept hooting like an owl." Debbie opened her eyes wide, and swiveled her head side to side until Tilly poked her in the ribs.

"I wasn't hooting," Tilly said. "I was asking 'où?' Everyone knows that means 'where' in French."

"Finally," Debbie went on, "our guide led Sis over to the stall he had been pointing at."

Tilly shrugged. "I thought truffles were chocolate."

"They're not?" Adelle asked. She loved chocolate truffles.

"They're fungi," Debbie said.

"You're a fun guy, too," groaned Tilly, rolling her eyes.

Even Barb smirked at that one.

"I googled them," Tilly said, emphasizing the "g" in google.

"You did?" Adelle was incredulous. "You're worse with technology than I am!"

"Barb showed me how," Tilly continued. "She lost our bet so she had to teach me something useful on her phone."

Barb chuckled. "I noticed she's been using a magnifying glass. The first lesson was how to use the zoom feature."

It was Tilly's turn to smirk. "I taught her a practical lesson, too."

This should be good.

Barb grinned. "I always wanted to learn how to knit." She looked at her mother and rolled her eyes. "Not."

The desserts were heavenly. Tilly had ordered two.

"I'm going to walk them off after dinner," she said, licking her spoon.

"Teresa would have loved the Saint Maurice Cathedral," exclaimed Debbie as she savored her chocolate soufflé.

Adelle noticed how deftly Evelyn changed the topic when Teresa's name came up. "Barb, what were you and Tilly betting about?" Evelyn asked her daughter.

Tilly sat up and answered first. "To see who could find the most passageways." She jerked her thumb at Barb. "Miss Smarty Pants kept getting lost. She always had her phone in her hands, and her head in the clouds."

The cloud!

If money was missing, reasoned Adelle, Barb should be able to use her computer skills to track it down by studying the financial statements. The income and expense statements were likely accessible in the cloud.

This is your chance, Adelle.

"Speaking of getting lost in passageways," began Adelle, "I have a question." The latest text from Wes had given her an idea. "I made a mistake using mobile banking, and sent my credit card payment to the wrong account." Wes had discovered the error on her statement. Adelle always paid her account in full every month. Always, that is, until now. She turned to Barb. "Where do you think my money is?" She paused for effect. "In the cloud somewhere?"

"As in 'flew away?'" Tilly asked, flapping her arms, winking at Debbie.

Barb smirked. "Cloud computing is an information technology paradigm—"

"Pair of dimes?" Tilly asked.

Debbie jumped in. "A paradigm is simply a way of looking at things. When you change the way you look at things, you're changing how you think about something."

Barb continued. "The technology paradigm enables ubiquitous access—"

Debbie winked at Adelle. "Who's big as us?" she asked Barb.

"Ubiquitous means being found everywhere at the same time," Barb said, sneering at Debbie. "The cloud gives access to shared pools of configurable system resources, and higher-level services that can be …"

As she tuned Barb out, Adelle noticed that Debbie was showing Evelyn how to make a swan with her napkin.

Adelle tuned back in when Tilly cleared her throat. "Should I use the cloud?"

"You need to understand the risks," Barb said. "Let's say we use Adelle's cabin as your cloud. Pretend it's a big storage box just for you. You can put your phone, your photo albums, your written list of passwords, and bank statements in her cabin."

Tilly nodded.

"Now imagine someone going into Adelle's cabin, and coming out looking exactly like you, carrying your stuff. She has all your information. She has stolen your identity."

Debbie laughed. "The world doesn't need two Tillys. One is enough!"

"Thanks, Sis."

As Barb tried to explain security issues to Tilly,

Debbie and Evelyn were laughing at their napkin art. Adelle noticed Barb twisting her own napkin.

Uh-oh ...

"So back to my bill payment," Adelle said. "I sent it to the wrong company. Where do you think it is?"

"At the wrong company." Barb stood up and tossed her napkin, now a white butterfly, at her mother. "See you girls at breakfast."

"Ask a stupid question, get a stupid answer," Tilly said, laughing at Adelle.

Adelle chuckled along with the other women, satisfied that she had planted a good clue. Until another thought occurred to her.

You can lead a horse to water, but you can't make it drink.

CHAPTER 4
TOURNON
ALL DOWNHILL FROM HERE

Tilly had the right idea, Adelle decided, as their ship docked in Tournon after dinner. A walk would be good after their scrumptious meal.

Walking down the ramp, Adelle was struck by the beauty surrounding them. They were docked beside a suspension bridge, linking Tournon to a delightful riverside town across the Rhône. She admired the steeply sloping vineyards overlooking the community. Pierre had told them that they had arrived in the center of an important wine-producing region known for its red Hermitage, white Larnarge, and Chante-Alouette wines. "Alouette, Jaunty Alouette," Debbie had sung. Now Adelle couldn't get that tune out of her head.

Adelle was pleased that Evelyn had joined them. She couldn't understand how Barb could spend most of her time in their cabin, working. Evelyn didn't seem to mind. She must be used to it, thought Adelle.

"Those are the most amazing trees I've ever seen,"

Evelyn observed as they strolled under the towering trees along the path into Tournon.

"They're plane trees," Debbie said.

Tilly frowned. "They are not plain, they are spectacular!"

Debbie laughed. "P-l-a-n-e, not p-l-a-i-n," she said, spelling each word. "They're related to our sycamore trees. Napoleon planted them throughout France so that his soldiers could rest in the shade."

Adelle pointed out a structure on the corner of the next street. "That looks interesting," she said.

"Looks plain to me," Tilly said, sticking her tongue out at her sister's back.

As they got nearer, they could see that the back and two sides of the structure were painted to look like full bookshelves. When they walked around to the front, they discovered a dozen books on the shelf inside.

"It's an old phone booth!" exclaimed Evelyn, clapping her hands. "They've made it into a lending library!" Of course, Adelle had to take a picture of the sisters squeezed inside.

The town was dominated by a dramatic feudal castle built on a granite rock. Another photo opportunity.

Debbie was anxious to return to the ship. She wanted a group photo on the suspension bridge before the sun went down. While Evelyn went to get Barb, Adelle and the sisters watched four elderly local men playing a game with bronze spheres the size of oranges.

"It's called boule lyonnaise, translated as the balls of Lyon," the ship's program director said as she arrived with Barb and Evelyn. The game reminded Adelle of bocce ball. One team threw a small wooden ball the size of a bottle cork onto the small gravel pad. Then the two teams took turns tossing the metal balls to see who could get closest. One team cheered as their player knocked the opponent's ball away. They turned and bowed as Debbie took a video.

The cable bridge connecting the towns of Tournon on the west bank with Tain-l'Hermitage on the east bank was named after French inventor Marc Seguin. In 1824, with the help of his brother, he had built the first bridge suspended from cables made of parallel wire strands. The current bridge was close to the site of the original suspension bridge.

Adelle was a little nervous. She could see the Rhône River below through the gaps in the wooden planks.

"Careful no one falls through the cracks," Debbie joked. "Smile!"

The next morning, Adelle settled into her train seat, looking forward to the steam train excursion through the Ardèche plateau.

Adelle scanned the Train de l'Ardèche brochure. The train was pulled by a Mallet locomotive, built to negotiate the tight curves in the gorge more easily. She looked at the map. They would follow the gorge through the Doux Valley, an untouched conservation area. Adelle learned that the restored locomotive had four double-acting pistons that were operated by steam from a coal-fired boiler. Skimming over the rest of the mechanical details, she was reminded of a former client. The first time she had met him, he seemed really cranky about investing. Finally, he had looked her in the eye, and gruffly asked her if she knew how to fix a diesel engine. When she told him she didn't, he said, "Then you do this, and I'll fix the engines." He turned into one of her favorite clients.

They were all your favorites.

Adelle felt a jolt as the train started to leave the station. She had a seat to herself in a carriage near the end of train. Thankfully she was facing forward, not like their local tour guide who was seated at the front, facing Adelle. Better her riding backwards than me, thought Adelle. She still had the odd bout of motion sickness. But never on the ship. Sometimes she couldn't tell if they were still docked, or sailing down the river again.

Adelle glanced at their guide. She was a dignified elderly woman, immaculately dressed, sitting with perfect posture, her silver hair done up in an elegant bun. In a thick French accent, she invited them to sit back and enjoy the view. She would begin her narration further along the route.

As the train slowly chugged up through the first bend, Adelle could see the black smoke from the engine ahead. Barb and Evelyn were seated in the first car with Debbie and Tilly. Everyone had been surprised at breakfast when Evelyn had announced that Barb was going to join them for the steam train tour. Adelle smiled contentedly. Barb must have found Teresa's funds in the cloud. Now she would be able to put her work away, and enjoy the trip with her mother.

Adelle listened attentively as their guide began her commentary. Their locomotive, a coal-fired steam engine, had been running on this route since 1903. The narrow-gauge track followed the gorge from Tournon on the Rhône River to Lamastre in the Doux Valley. It was thirty-three kilometers, or twenty-one miles, long. The line originally opened in 1891 to supply milk and wood to Tournon, and was now a popular tourist attraction. Adelle could understand why. The beautiful Ardèche countryside was spectacular. She admired the steep hills blanketed by tall green trees and jagged outcroppings.

After clattering through a short tunnel, the guide advised that the train would travel over three viaducts, a specific type of bridge built by using arches. They would also pass an ancient Roman aqueduct.

The aqueducts were designed and built to supply fresh clean water for drinking, fountains, and Roman baths, using gravity and the natural slope of the land. Given that most of the Roman aqueducts were built more than two thousand years ago and many were still standing, they were exceptional feats of engineering for their time. Adelle was surprised to learn that the Romans used stone, brick, and volcanic cement in their construction. *Cement?*

The guide must have noticed Adelle's reaction. "Tomorrow you will be in Viviers. When you go up the hill to the cathedral for your night walk, you should be able to see the lights of the Lafarge cement plant across the Rhône." The worldwide industrial company had been founded in 1833 by Joseph-Auguste Pavin de Lafarge near a large limestone quarry.

The train stopped at a small station for a short break.

"You're not taking pictures like everyone else?" Adelle asked Evelyn, standing between the train and the gorge.

"I don't have my phone with me," Evelyn replied, grinning. "I made a bet with Barb that the two of us couldn't be away from our cell phones for the morning, but she surprised me. She left her phone in our cabin and I lost the bet."

"She's here without her phone?" Adelle couldn't believe it. "What did it cost you?"

Evelyn laughed. "You will never guess what I'll be doing later."

Adelle didn't have the foggiest idea.

"Knitting comfort dolls!"

When the steam train reached the next station, all the passengers were asked to disembark. They watched as the uncoupled locomotive steamed forward onto a side track. Then it backed up onto a short set of tracks in the middle of a circular turntable. Adelle was amazed when the engineer jumped down from the locomotive, then singlehandedly pushed the locomotive around in the circle until it was facing the opposite direction. He climbed back up, and with a cheery blast from the steam whistle, the locomotive chugged to the back of the train, which now became the front.

"That was the neatest thing I've ever seen," gushed Evelyn. "Did you see how that man turned that heavy locomotive all by himself?"

Debbie was equally impressed. She wanted a picture of her and Tilly standing beside the turntable. Barb volunteered to take the photo, and Debbie handed Barb her phone.

"It's incredible the fool didn't drop it into the gorge," Tilly said, describing how her sister had leaned out the open window of their carriage for most of the trip to video their tour. She stood beside Debbie and grimaced.

"Smile, Tilly," Debbie said. "It's all downhill from here!"

"Can I use your phone for a moment?" Barb asked Debbie afterward.

Evelyn rolled her eyes when Barb turned and walked away, thumbs flying.

"Any good news?" Adelle asked Evelyn before they boarded the train for the ride back. Evelyn shook her head. The funds were still missing.

Adelle was disappointed that her idea hadn't helped. She had been so sure that Barb's expertise with technology would detect anomalies in the financial statements. Like the Romans, Barb was a genius. Evelyn had confirmed it. She was proud of her daughter. "She always had the highest marks in school. Although we were never quite sure how she got there."

Tilly was less impressed by Barb's technology wizardry. Especially when Barb got lost in the covered passageways of Lyon. "Barb," Tilly had teased, "you have to be smarter than your smart phone."

As the train passed the aqueduct again, Adelle's thoughts strayed to its purpose, carrying water to communities.

Water going in, water going out.

The train clattered back through the short tunnel. Coming out into the bright sunshine, Adelle squinted at the gorge below. She marveled at how long it would have taken the river to chisel it out, a little at a time, slowly, each and every day. She imagined time lapse photography illustrating how the gorge was formed. Like they did with storms on the Weather Channel.

The Weather Channel? Focus, you old geezer.

Adelle retraced her thinking.

Water going in, water going out.

Receivables coming in, expenses going out.

Adelle recalled working with young clients. She had often explained budgeting in a simple way. They didn't need to spend money and time on fancy software to get a handle on their finances. It wasn't about their income and expenses. It was about their savings. If their savings were going down, they were spending more than they made. If their savings were going up, they were spending less than their income. If spending equaled income, their budget was balanced.

Balanced.

Balance sheets!

She wondered if Barb had done a comparative analysis of the corporate balance sheets.

Adelle sat up. Now that she had another clue for Barb to investigate, Adelle wondered how best to share it. Should she be patient and hope Barb figured it out on her own? Or should she break her promise to not get involved? Or was there another way? What if she could convince Evelyn to let her back out of her promise, like the locomotive, backing onto the turntable and changing directions?

Adelle tried, but she couldn't come up with any other viable ideas. The river cruise was half over, and Barb hadn't found the funds yet. Teresa needed help. It was time to get involved. After all, the situation couldn't get any worse.

Could it?

Barb was standing on the platform as Adelle gathered her things and waited her turn to get off the train. Adelle pretended to stumble on the last step. "Sorry," she said, reaching for Barb's outstretched arm. "I lost my balance." She grabbed Barb's hand. "I'm always losing my balance."

Nothing.

Barb was shifting from foot to foot. She wanted to trade places with Adelle for the shuttle ride back to the ship. Adelle took pity on her and agreed. She knew Barb was anxious to get back to work.

Back in her cabin onboard the ship, Adelle was relieved to find that the honey and jam jars fit into her carry-on luggage. She had purchased the small containers from local farmers at the Ardèche train station. Adelle was proud that she only ever traveled with carry-on, much to the consternation of many of her friends. They could do it, too, if they packed coordinated, wrinkle-free outfits that could be rolled. And only packed one extra pair of sensible shoes that would go with everything. And left all their extra hair product at home.

Although it would have been nice to take a few more gifts home ...

As Adelle stored her carry-on back in her closet, she heard a sharp knock on her cabin door. She looked through the peephole, and saw a red-faced Barb.

"Why weren't you watching out for my mother?" Barb demanded, as she pushed her way into the cabin. She turned and glared at Adelle, hands on her hips. "She didn't come back."

"What?"

"Are you losing it, too? My mother is missing!"

Evelyn was missing? The last time Adelle had noticed her was when the train had turned around at the top of the gorge.

"When was the last time you saw her?" Adelle asked, fighting to keep her voice steady.

"When I left her at the train station with you."

Uh-oh.

Adelle had assumed that Evelyn had returned to the ship on the shuttle with Barb. When the shuttle driver's count was off at the train station, Adelle had reassured him that she had switched places with two other passengers. He was free to leave and return to the ship.

Barb was furious. "You assumed wrong. She didn't check back in."

That wasn't good. When passengers left the ship, they were each given their identity card. It was to be returned to the reception desk when they came back onboard.

Adelle was tempted to point out that she wasn't the only one who had made a wrong assumption. Barb had obviously assumed Evelyn was with Adelle.

That's not the point, Adelle. Evelyn is missing. You're the tour host. Do something.

Before Adelle could respond, Barb stormed out the door.

An anxious hour later, Adelle was relieved to see Evelyn standing on the deck, staring at the countryside as their ship sailed down the Rhône. She needed to talk to her friend to see what had happened. As Adelle approached from behind, Evelyn hung her head. Adelle felt sorry for her. She decided to give Evelyn a moment to collect herself. Evelyn looked up, then back down. Again, and again.

Adelle realized that Evelyn was watching a woman who was seated at a table by the railing, posture erect, staring intently at the shore.

Adelle crept up to Evelyn to see what was going on. "What's happening?" she whispered.

Evelyn raised her finger to her lips as she pointed

over the woman's shoulder. "She's painting."

Adelle took a step sideways to see better. On the table, she saw a coiled sketchbook open to a blank page, an unzipped pouch containing pencils and paint brushes, a glass of water, and a small spritz bottle. She moved over a little, and saw an open travel paint box, which was roughly the size of a cell phone. It held twelve solid, stamp-sized blocks of paint in various hues. Two small white mixing palettes were attached to the paint box.

The artist hadn't moved. "What is she staring at?" Adelle whispered, looking at the shore. All she could see were rows and rows of vineyards on the hillsides.

Evelyn shrugged her shoulders and shook her head.

Finally, the artist selected a pencil from the pouch, and quickly drew a flat line across the bottom third of the page. She added two swooping curves above the line. Then she penciled in a stone hut and wall. Adelle scoured the countryside for the hut, but they must have sailed past it already. She looked back at the artist's sketchbook, where a colorful painting was already emerging.

While the artist continued to paint quickly, Adelle's curiosity got the best of her.

"What happened?" she whispered in Evelyn's ear. "How did you get back to the ship?"

"I missed the shuttle," replied Evelyn quietly. "The guide drove me back."

Before Adelle could ask any more questions, it started to rain and everyone scattered.

CHAPTER 5

VIVIERS

LIFE IS SIMPLER THAN WE MAKE IT

"The gall!" Tilly exclaimed as Adelle sat down at the dinner table that night.

This should be good.

"What do you mean, Sis?" Debbie asked. She turned to Adelle, shrugging her shoulders. "All I did was ask her if she knew who ruled this area before the Romans."

"Now we're even." Tilly winked at Adelle. "The Gaul. G-a-u-l, not g-a-l-l."

Adelle laughed, wondering what it had been like when the sisters were little girls, never mind seniors!

"How do you know that?" Debbie challenged.

"I googled it," Tilly boasted.

"You're just like a reformed smoker, only in reverse," Debbie said, chuckling. "First you put technology down, and now you're on it all the time."

"Not quite," Tilly said. "Only when I need it." Tilly raised her wine in salute. "Everything in moderation, including moderation."

Tilly would make a good tour host, Adelle thought as she listened to what Tilly had learned about their next port. Viviers was one of the remaining walled communities of Europe, perched on a hill overlooking the Rhône valley. The walls were built to protect the village throughout the Hundred Years' War between France and England during the Middle Ages.

Tilly had reviewed their ship's daily newsletter as well. "After dinner, there's a walking tour through the lower town, then up to the upper town where Saint Vincent's cathedral looks over Viviers and the Rhône. It's said to be the smallest active cathedral in France."

Debbie chuckled. "ABC, another bloody cathedral!"

"I read that it dates back to the twelfth century," Tilly said, ignoring her sister. "Something about a blend of different architectural styles."

Once again, Adelle was reminded of Teresa. She wished she could help. She glanced at Barb, who was pecking away at her phone. She obviously thought they were too old to be useful.

The gall.

Adelle turned her attention to her menu. She wondered if she should start with prawns with garlic and olive oil, or the sweet peas veloute, whatever that was, and curried shrimp. She cringed when Tilly read the beef main course out loud. "Boeuf Wellington Decompose."

Decomposed Beef Wellington?

"Deconstructed beef Wellington with roasted mushroom and truffle jus," Debbie said, reading the English small print.

"Deconstructed?" Adelle was puzzled.

Evelyn explained that deconstructing food meant breaking apart the components that were traditionally combined to make a dish, and serving the items separately in a unique way.

Tilly smirked. "Like serving Barb's burger patty beside the bun, beside the pickle, beside the butter. At home, we call that 'build your own burger.'"

Adelle scanned the desserts section. She wanted to make sure to save room for the chocolate soufflé afterward. She chuckled, remembering what her grandson always said. "Don't worry Grandma, I won't be too full. There's a special place in my stomach for dessert."

During their appetizers, Tilly continued to share what she had discovered about Viviers.

"It's one of the best-preserved medieval towns in the south of France. I read that the population was thirty thousand in medieval times, but now it's around four thousand."

Debbie eyes sparkled. "I bet we'll see ghosts on our night walk."

Ghosts. Adelle had been haunted by something Barb had said earlier. She just couldn't remember what it was.

Adelle heard Tilly clear her throat. *Focus, Adelle.*

"The reviewers summed up Viviers as a tiny village, lost in its own world," Tilly said. She laughed. "Like Adelle."

Lost ... losing ... losing it!

Barb had implied that Evelyn and Adelle were both losing it!

Just then, the servers converged on their table with their main course. Adelle was impressed by her beef Wellington. It was a work of art, beef resting on a bed of mushrooms peeking out from under a pastry pinwheel. It almost looked too good to eat. *Almost.*

"Mother!" Barb exclaimed when the server set Evelyn's plate in front of her. "You ordered fish!" Her voice cracked. "You never eat fish. You don't like fish."

"It's good for the brain," declared Evelyn, picking up her cutlery.

Did she just wink at Tilly?

Barb threw her napkin down on the table, as she shoved her chair back. "That's it, you're moving to the coast with me."

"What?" Evelyn dropped her fork, wide-eyed. "Why?"

What is going on?

Tilly looked at Evelyn. "What about your gentleman friend?"

Gentleman friend?

Barb glared at her mother. "What gentleman friend?"

"Annie …" Evelyn moaned. "I was going to tell you …"

Barb stood abruptly and turned to leave.

Before she could stop herself, Adelle blurted, "You can't leave now. We need to talk about helping Teresa."

Barb stopped in her tracks. She glared at her mother.

Then she whirled around and glared at Adelle. "It's too late. Teresa is filing for creditor protection on Monday." Barb marched out the door.

Evelyn jumped up and ran after her.

Creditor protection?

"Well," Tilly said, buttering a piece of her bun. "That was awkward."

"That's all you have to say for yourself?" Debbie demanded.

Tilly bit into her bun, followed by a sip of wine. "It's not my fault. Everyone knows I can't keep a secret."

Adelle slumped into her chair.

Neither can you, Adelle.

Adelle trailed behind the small group as they followed the local tour guide through the lower town of Viviers. Neither Barb nor Evelyn had shown up for the night walk.

As their hushed group trekked single file up another narrow cobblestone street, the few scattered lights produced an eerie glow. The shutters were closed on the solid stone medieval buildings. The streets were deserted. Adelle shuddered when a black cat ran across her path.

Way to go, Adelle.

She had failed miserably. She had led Barb astray, chasing Adelle's stupid ideas about the cloud and balance sheets. Valuable time had been wasted. Teresa was on the verge of bankruptcy. On top of that, Barb held her responsible for temporarily losing her mother. She didn't trust Adelle any more. Worse yet, she had broken her promise to Evelyn not to let on that she knew Barb was working for Teresa. Adelle would never forget the look of dismay on Evelyn's face when she raced after her daughter.

In upper Viviers, they passed the closed cathedral and walked under a stone arch passageway into a court-yard overlooking the Rhône valley below.

"There's a UFO," Adelle heard Tilly say. There were bright lights clustered at a distance across the valley. The guide reassured them it was the Lafarge facility.

Was that thunder? Adelle froze. She was terrified of thunderstorms. She always had been, ever since she was a young girl. She remembered her mother gathering her and her younger sister and brother together in her moth-er's bed, pulling the blankets over the four of them until the storm was over.

A flash of lightning lit up the courtyard.

One Mississippi, two Mississippi ... Adelle breathed a sigh of relief when she counted ten Mississippis before she heard the long roll of the thunder.

"Are you okay?"

Adelle jumped straight up. *Breathe, Adelle, breathe.*

Just then, the sky lit up again to reveal Debbie standing beside her. They counted out loud together, Debbie more enthusiastically than Adelle.

Phew! It's still far away. Maybe it will skirt around us.

Debbie loved thunderstorms. "When we were kids, Tilly and I would stand at the window and marvel at Mother Nature's free light and sound show. Dad told us that the rain meant the crops and gardens would grow, and Mom said—"

The lightning flashed again.

One Mississippi, two Mississ—

BOOM!

Adelle turned and ran.

Adelle clutched the bed covers under her chin. The thunder had stopped.

It's all Teresa's fault, she thought. If she had come on this trip as planned, she would have kept Barb company. Everyone would be happy.

But Teresa didn't come. Barb's mother came instead.

Lovely Evelyn, recalled Adelle. The perfect replacement.

Until she told you that Barb was working for Teresa. And made you promise not to tell.

Adelle moaned. She had broken her promise.

In front of Evelyn. And Debbie. And Tilly.

"I can't help it," Adelle told her conscience. "Despite my good intentions, I always fail, and then I always feel guilty."

And keep us both awake.

"What should I do now?"

First, apologize to Evelyn.

"She's lovely, she'll forgive me."

Second, talk to Barb.

"Do I have to?"

You're the one who wants to help Teresa.

"Okay, okay."

Adelle still couldn't sleep. The dinner scene kept playing over and over in her mind. She finally got up, dressed, and went out to the lounge. To her surprise, Mickey was sitting in the far corner.

"Can't sleep either?" she asked her friend.

"I just finished giving my presentation on Zoom," Mickey replied. "It's the afternoon back home."

Adelle couldn't believe what she was hearing. *Mickey used Zoom?* Sure enough, the page with the red heart, stick man, cloud, and question mark were on the table in front of Mickey, beside her phone.

Mickey's red crayon rolled off the table, and Adelle stooped to pick it up. That's when she saw the white cane resting beside Mickey's chair.

Mickey is blind?

Adelle sat back up, and waved the red crayon in front of Mickey's eyes.

Mickey snatched it away, laughing. "Quit teasing me, that's mine."

Adelle was too tired to couch her words. "I was checking to see if you're blind."

"Blind? Why?"

Adelle pointed under Mickey's chair. "I saw your white cane."

Mickey laughed. "That's not a cane. It's my extendible selfie stick! Luckily, Evelyn found it for me. I had left it on the train when we were in Ardèche."

That's why Evelyn missed the shuttle.

When Mickey asked Adelle why she was up in the middle of the night, Adelle told her everything. From gossiping about Barb, inadvertently trashing her to her mother of all people, to breaking all her promises, and failing miserably as a tour guide.

Mickey listened patiently, then reached out and took Adelle's hand. She looked directly into Adelle's eyes. "A friend taught me something that I'm going to pass on to you. I think it will help."

Adelle needed all the help she could get.

"Be careful how you think. Your thoughts shape your life."

Back in bed, Adelle thought about Mickey's advice.

You think you are old and useless.

Adelle wondered when she had started to think like that. She wanted to blame Barb's old geezer comment, but she knew that wasn't right. It had started when she was still working. Technology was changing faster than she could keep up. It was so frustrating. Although there had been some comical times. When her partners convinced her to use a phone headset, for example. They had set it up for her, and coached her how to use it. She remembered putting it on for the first time, and anxiously waiting for the next call. The phone rang. She pushed the button. Nothing happened. "This stupid thing doesn't work," she had blurted. "Adelle," she heard on her headset, "you're supposed to say hello first." Thankfully, it was Wes.

What would Wes say about the mess she found herself in now? He'd probably say "Pumpkin ..." She loved it when he called her pumpkin, as long as he didn't say it in public. When they had first met, they were listening to a radio show when a caller phoned in to request a song for his girlfriend of two weeks. When the announcer asked him what his girlfriend's name was, the caller replied, "I don't know. I just call her Pumpkin."

She knew what Wes would say. "Pumpkin, relax." She tried. It didn't help.

When did she get so *old?*

A little every day. Like the gorge.

That thinking didn't help either.

Back up, like the locomotive. Turn your thinking around. Reverse it all.

Adelle was stuck. How could she think younger when she felt so ancient?

Mickey's young at heart. Age is just a number.

Adelle remembered Mickey's parting words before they said goodnight. "Life is simpler than we make it, Adelle." Maybe Adelle had blown everything out of proportion. What if Evelyn was wrong? What if Barb wanted help?

You won't know until you ask.

But what if they couldn't solve the mystery of the missing funds?

You won't know until you try.

Okay, okay, I'll keep trying.

Finally.

Good night.

CHAPTER 6
ARLES
VOILA

The next morning, Adelle woke up alert and reenergized. And late. She had slept so soundly that she had missed her alarm, missed breakfast, and almost missed the last group heading out on the walking tour of Arles. Her apologies and inquiries would have to wait until lunch.

Their local guide was delightful. Adelle learned that the Romans had arrived in Arles in 123 BC. They had expanded the settlement into an important trading city. At first it was overshadowed by the coastal port of Marseille, but that changed when civil war broke out amongst the Romans from 49 BC to 45 BC. Marseille sided with Pompey while Arles chose his rival, and ultimate victor, Julius Caesar. All the treasures from Marseille were then transferred to Arles.

Adelle was surprised to hear that Arles had been a big retirement center for retired soldiers of the Roman legions. After signing up and serving for twenty years, the soldiers were usually awarded land or a large sum of money. That explained why the army was made up of trained and experienced solders, Adelle thought. *Clever.*

Close to Arles, the Romans had milled flour from wheat, using an aqueduct and sixteen water wheels. The site was regarded as one of the first industrial complexes in human history. Adelle made a mental note to mention this in her next text to Wes.

Adelle couldn't get over the size of the prominent two-tiered Roman amphitheater in the heart of Arles. It was encircled by one hundred and twenty imposing Romanesque arches dating back to the first century AD. The arena had once seated more than twenty thousand spectators, who were entertained by chariot races and armed combatants in violent confrontations.

Confrontation. Not your forte, Adelle.

Adelle laughed at her instinctive fear of confrontation. Barb might be combative sometimes, but she wasn't armed. *Or was she?* She had more technology expertise at her disposal.

You have more people experience.

With the fall of the empire in the fifth century, the oval arena became a shelter for the city's population. It was transformed into a fortress with four towers, three of which were still standing. Over two hundred houses and two chapels were protected inside. It wasn't until 1830 that Roman events were once again held in the amphitheater.

Two blocks away from the arena, they found them-selves in the center of the old town. Their tour guide led them into the public lobby of the old city hall, built in 1675, then out another door into a large plaza. They were facing the church of Saint Trophime, built between the twelfth and fifteenth centuries. Its façade, made up of sculptures depicting various biblical scenes, had been declared a UNESCO World Heritage site.

Next, they wandered through the ruins of Le Theatre Antique, now a reconstructed Roman theater. It was built by Julius Caesar a century before the larger amphitheater. Like the bigger arena, it was still being used, now for dance and music shows and an annual film festival. There used to be a back wall to enhance the acoustics, but now only two remaining columns survived, known locally as the "two widows."

Adelle wished she could have apologized to Evelyn that morning.

That was then, this is now. Enjoy the tour, you will see her later.

The next stop was the Roman thermal baths, an enormous spa complex that had been built by Emperor Constantine in the fourth century AD at the peak of the Roman empire. The water came to Arles from the low mountains south of Arles via an aqueduct into a tank, and was then distributed throughout the community via lead pipes. While the wealthy Romans had small bath-houses built into their mansions, the public baths were a center of the daily Roman social scene. Most afternoons people went to bathe, exercise, and socialize before their evening meal. The baths consisted of various sections, including a changing room, an exercise area, a cold-water pool, a warm room, and a hot room which was heated by a subfloor heating system.

Heated floors. In the fourth century AD!

The excursion concluded at the Arles hospital, built in the sixteenth and seventeenth centuries, and famous for its most well-known patient, Vincent Van Gogh. The painter moved to Arles in February of 1888 because he appreciated the "vivid colors and strong compositional outlines" of Provence. During his time there, he produced more than two hundred paintings, including *The Starry Night, Café de Nuit*, and *The Sunflowers*. By December of that year, his mental health had deterio-rated, and after cutting off his own left ear following an altercation with the painter Paul Gauguin, he was hospi-talized. Twice. He left Arles in May of 1889.

The complex had operated as a hospital into the 1970s and was now a cultural space, home to an art gallery, restaurants, shops, and the beautiful courtyard gardens.

Adelle was in her happy place. She had thoroughly enjoyed the tour.

Adelle found Debbie and Tilly eating a late lunch on the ship's deck.

"What happened to you this morning?" Debbie asked, as Adelle sat down to join them.

"I slept in," she admitted. "Where are Evelyn and Barb?"

"Barb's working," Debbie replied. "Remember the painter you and Evelyn met on the deck? She and Evelyn went on the optional Van Gogh excursion."

Adelle was grateful for the opportunity to apologize to the sisters for the commotion she had caused at dinner the previous night.

"Girls, I'm sorry for blurting last night," she began.

"Don't be sorry," protested Debbie. "I love your blurts!"

"You do?" This was easier than Adelle had expected.

"You've given me some great ideas for my store, and Tilly said you gave her some good ideas, too."

"I did?"

"Don't let your head get too swelled," Tilly said, rolling her eyes at her sister. "Our local town has a run-down vacant lot on Main Street. Your idea about sprucing up Debbie's coffee space got me to thinking. We could plant grass and flowers on that lot, paint a mural on the building beside it, and add some shade trees."

Adelle experienced a warm fuzzy feeling. Every now and then, one of her ideas worked out. Maybe she could garden after all.

Evelyn. The warm fuzzies disappeared.

"Why didn't anyone tell me that Evelyn had a gentleman friend?"

"It's your own fault," Tilly said, taking a sip of water. "You don't like gossip."

"There's a big difference between gossip and the need to know!" Adelle cried.

"Evelyn and I had a chat in the lounge last night," Debbie shared. "Before this trip, she wasn't sure if she was ready to pursue another relationship. That's why she hadn't said anything to Barb."

"How did you find out?" Adelle still wished Evelyn had confided in *her*.

"Miss Rubberneck," Debbie answered, pointing at Tilly. "She overheard her chatting with him on the phone."

Tilly sniffed. "Thanks to me, Miss All About Fashion here has been giving her a makeover."

Adelle realized that Evelyn was no longer the frumpy, timid woman she had met only a few days ago.

"I convinced her to part her hair on the other side," Debbie boasted. "It gives it more volume. And I talked her into wearing a little makeup."

Adelle had a fleeting memory of mascara under Evelyn's eyes after the impromptu "Ave Maria" performance.

Tilly laughed. "At first I teased Evelyn that she was all painted up like a floozy, but she's getting the hang of it now."

"I talked her into buying some leggings," Debbie

said. "Maureen had warned her about all the delicious food, so all she had packed were her fat pants."

"Fat pants?" Adelle asked.

"You know," Debbie replied. "The pants every woman has in her closet in case she gains weight again. They were practically falling off thanks to Miss All About Aging Better and her exercising and eating tips."

Tilly chuckled. "She needs to work on using her non-dominant hand better."

Is she right-handed, or left-handed?

"After Vienne," Debbie continued, "she decided that she was ready to take the next step. She said you had helped her. Something about her husband and their song always being their song."

"Ave Maria."

Debbie's eyes glistened. "I think she was waiting for the perfect time to tell Barb."

And me, thought Adelle.

It's not always about you, Adelle.

"Why is Barb insisting Evelyn move back with her?" Adelle asked.

"She thinks her mother is losing it."

"That's ridiculous," Tilly chimed in. "There's nothing wrong with her." She put her fork down, shifted in her seat, looked at Adelle and then at Debbie.

"What?" Debbie asked.

"I know the real reason she wants to move her mother in with her."

"Spill, Sis."

"It's gossip."

Adelle grinned. "Spill, Tilly."

"Barb's pregnant."

Pregnant?

"Barbara, we need to talk."

Breathe, Adelle, breathe. Look confident.

"Now."

It was only after Adelle sat down on one of the single beds in Barb and Evelyn's cabin that she noticed Barb's runny nose and red eyes. She was clutching one of Tilly's comfort dolls to her chest. Adelle's firm resolve evaporated. "What's wrong?"

"You wouldn't understand."

Patience, Adelle.

"Give me a chance. Try me."

"I thought I could do this by myself, but I can't."

Poor thing!

"Your mother can help."

"She doesn't have the capacity," Barb stammered, tears sliding down her face.

"What?" Adelle was confused.

"Don't you see? She's losing it."

"Because she's eating fish?"

"It's not just that." Barb counted on her fingers as she described all of Evelyn's inconsistencies. New clothes, colorful silk scarves.

"And now leggings," Barb added, closing her eyes and scrunching her shoulders.

Silently, Adelle agreed. Leggings were for trim figures like Barb's.

"She's even wearing makeup." Barb scowled at Adelle. "What did you say to her in Vienne? She came back to the cabin with mascara running down her face."

Adelle grimaced. She was going to tell Evelyn about it, but something had distracted her. *Again.*

"She never wears lipstick," Barb continued. "Now she smears it all around her mouth. She turns the wrong way every time she leaves the restaurant. No wonder she missed the shuttle back from the train tour." Barb scowled again. "Not that you were any help."

Adelle flinched.

Time to change tactics.

"Barb, I can see you're upset. It's probably just your hormones."

Barb glared at Adelle. "My hormones?"

Adelle swallowed. She was making a mess of this. It was time to face the music. "I know about your baby."

Barb looked shocked. "My baby?" She clutched the doll tighter, and closed her eyes. "Is everybody losing it?"

"Pardon?"

Barb glared at Adelle again. "Haven't you listened to anything I've said? My mother is losing it. Rapidly."

"What are you talking about?" It was Adelle's turn to get upset. "There's nothing wrong with Evelyn." *Or the rest of us.*

"Haven't you noticed the drooling?" Barb started to pace. She whirled around, and shook the wool doll at

Adelle. "Wait. You did. You were all laughing at her. Laughing!"

Adelle struggled to figure out what Barb was talking about.

She spilled her soup when she was using her wrong hand.

Like a flash of lightning, it all became clear. "I can explain everything."

Adelle took a deep breath.

"When you saw her drooling, she was trying to eat her soup with her wrong hand. We weren't laughing at her, we were laughing with her."

"Why would she do that?"

"Tilly has been teaching her tips to help her age more gracefully. Like using her nondominant hand to eat her soup. Or comb her hair. Or brush her teeth."

Barb frowned. "Most mornings she has toothpaste all over her face."

Adelle continued. "We've all tried to find alternate ways to our cabins. Tilly says it's good exercise for our brains."

As Adelle told Barb about Debbie's makeover efforts and Tilly's suggestions for healthier food choices, Barb relaxed her grip on her comfort doll.

"What about missing the shuttle?"

"She didn't tell you the reason?" *Of course not.* Adelle knew her friend would protect Mickey from any embarrassment. But Barb needed to know. Adelle told her how Evelyn had gone back to the train for Mickey's selfie stick.

"That's my mom," Barb boasted, sitting up straighter. "Always looking out for others." She wiped her tears away and looked up, lips quivering. "But why was she crying in Vienne?"

"I should have told her about the mascara, but I was distracted and forgot."

"You're pretty easily distracted," Barbara observed. "But it still doesn't answer my question."

Adelle, you promised not to tell.

"Barb, I think the bottom line is that your mother loves you very much. To the moon and back, she told me. She didn't want you to know why she was upset because she knew the reason would upset you as well."

"Tell me. I need to know."

She's right.

As Adelle told Barb about the beautiful rendition of "Ave Maria," tears once again slid down the young woman's cheeks. Adelle reached out and patted her arm. "It's okay. You don't want to upset the baby."

Barb burst out laughing. "Trust me, Adelle. I'm not having a baby."

They heard a noise in the hallway outside the cabin door.

Adelle put her finger to her lips, and tiptoed over to look out the peephole.

"Voilà," Adelle announced, jerking the door open. Debbie and Tilly tumbled into the cabin.

Debbie had the grace to be embarrassed, but Tilly was defiant. "How else are we going to find out what's going on?" she insisted.

When Barb had stopped laughing, she asked Tilly why she thought she was pregnant.

"I overheard you on your phone. You said your AI project was affirmative," Tilly replied, arms crossed.

"AI?" Adelle asked.

Tilly stared at Adelle. "Artificial insemination. Everyone knows that."

"Oh, Sis …" Debbie groaned. "AI also stands for artificial intelligence. It refers to computers creating programs to mimic human thinking."

"Human thinking?" Tilly rolled her eyes. "What is so intelligent about that?"

She has a good point.

Barb started to explain that she was using artificial intelligence to find hidden and implicit correlations in data.

"Teresa may have been hacked," Adelle interpreted.

"Hacked?" Tilly cried. "Is she okay?"

Barbara smirked. "Her company may have been hacked. Hacked means gaining unauthorized access to data in a system."

Unauthorized access. Adelle's fingers started to tingle.

"Teresa has given me access to all of her records, and I've been looking for anything that looks out of the ordinary."

Think, Adelle. Was there anything new with Teresa since our first trip?

Something twigged. It was a long shot. Adelle remembered that on the first trip, Teresa was going to replace a key employee who was retiring. There was someone new on the job.

Adelle had an idea. "Barb, are you working directly with Teresa?"

"No, her accountant."

"What if it's someone on the inside? With authorized access?" Adelle asked.

Barb stopped pacing.

After Adelle shared her theory of what could have happened to the missing funds, Barb sat down and opened her laptop.

"I need to get to work." But before Adelle and the sisters had time to leave, Barb slammed the cover shut.

"What's wrong?" Adelle asked. Barb was clearly upset.

"I can't remember the password to my passwords," Barb admitted, eyes filling with tears again.

"Maybe you're the one who is losing it," Tilly teased.

Adelle held her breath.

Barb *laughed.*

How does Tilly get away with that? Adelle wondered.

More importantly, why can't Barb remember her password?

Adelle tried to put herself in Barb's place. She had been under a lot of stress.

Think, Adelle. Think.

Bingo.

"Barb, would you like us to find your mother and explain what has happened?"

Barb closed her eyes.

Is she going to cry again?

Suddenly, she opened her laptop and her fingers began to fly.

"Got it." She looked up at Adelle and smiled. "Yes, please. Thank you."

CHAPTER 7
AVIGNON

WITH A LITTLE HELP FROM MY FRIENDS

Adelle, Debbie, and Tilly waited eagerly for Barb and Evelyn to join them for breakfast. Because of the time difference, Barb had needed to work all night, and was likely sleeping in. Adelle hoped their theory about the missing funds was correct.

"Can you explain to us what Barb is doing?" Tilly asked, crossing her arms. "I asked her, but she told me I wouldn't understand."

Adelle smiled. It had been an interesting twenty-four hours. She and the sisters had gone back into Arles to meet Evelyn at the conclusion of her Van Gogh painting excursion. They persuaded her to join them for coffee.

You bribed her with chocolate croissants.

"So much for all my talk about healthy eating," Tilly had grumbled. Once they had explained all the misunderstandings to Evelyn, Adelle ordered another round of croissants.

At dinner, Evelyn had stopped by their table long

enough to tell them that she was taking food back to the cabin to share with Barb. When Adelle asked her if Barb was making progress, Evelyn smiled. "Affirmative."

Tilly asked you a question.

Adelle considered telling Tilly the truth. One of the breakthrough clues was Debbie's wisecrack that one Tilly was enough.

That's not very nice. Think again.

Adelle took another moment to think.

Duplicates.

Bingo!

"Tilly, you supplied the main clue," Adelle began. "Do you remember when you were telling us earlier in the trip how eager you were to tour Avignon?"

Tilly nodded.

"And sharing your research about the duplicate Popes?"

Tilly had read that Pope Clement V had moved to Avignon in 1309 because he was unwilling to face the violent chaos in Rome after his election. A succession of Popes continued to reside In Avignon for the next sixty years. Then there was a split in the Catholic Church from 1378 until 1417. Two men each claimed to be the true Pope.

"Duplicate Popes," Adelle repeated. "If the missing funds were due to internal fraud and the new accountant, perhaps there was a duplicate set of books."

Tilly sat back, beaming.

"Evelyn said I helped, too," Debbie reminded them, pretending to pout. "How?"

Adelle chuckled to herself. Debbie's annoying habit of feeding her social media accounts had paid dividends.

"Before we contacted Teresa with our suspicions, we checked out the accountant on social media. His posts showed an increasing life of luxury." Armed with this information, Barb had contacted Teresa directly and provided her with the financial statements the accountant had made available. It didn't take long for Teresa to confirm that there were two sets of records.

"Bottom line, the accountant had overreported the expenses and underreported the revenues, then skimmed the difference into various holding company bank accounts, all controlled by him. Barb is trying to track down the funds."

Adelle studied the breakfast menu. The eggs Benedict with hollandaise was calling her name.

"Good morning, girls," Evelyn said, pulling out a chair.

"Where's Barb?" Tilly asked.

"Did she find the money yet?" Debbie wanted to know.

Evelyn held up her hands and shrugged. Barb was back in their cabin, waiting for final confirmation. "She said she hoped to join us later on our walking tour."

"Avignon would make an excellent backdrop for a medieval fairy tale," Evelyn whispered to Adelle as they followed their local tour guide the short distance from their ship to the main gate.

"Not only did this fortified wall protect Avignon from invaders in the Middle Ages," their guide began, "it also protected the town from modernization. The old town is well preserved with large pedestrian zones and historic buildings and monuments." The guide looked at Debbie, who was busy taking pictures. "For the photographers in the group, be sure you walk back and take a photo here tonight. The lighting on the wall is spectacular."

Not far inside the main gate, they entered a large square in front of the massive limestone Palace of the Popes.

"This is today's largest surviving Gothic palace in Europe," the guide proudly informed them. Tilly poked Debbie when their guide told them that Avignon was famous in the fourteenth century as the "other Rome." A French Pope had been elected in 1309, and had decided that Italy was too dangerous, so he moved the whole operation to Avignon, under the support of the French king.

"Avignon was a nothing town at the time," the guide said. "The Catholic church literally bought it and gave it a makeover."

Debbie winked at Adelle.

"The Church created vast spaces for public squares, this palace, mansions for cardinals, and residences for the entire bureaucracy. As the population went from six thousand to twenty-five thousand, they built this large protective wall around the community."

Barb has a protective wall, too, Adelle thought.

As Tilly says, you spot it, you got it.

Adelle agreed with her conscience. *Touché.*

"In all, seven Popes ruled from Avignon, making it the center of Christianity for one hundred years. Meanwhile, the Italians demanded an Italian Pope, so from 1378 to 1417 there were twin Popes."

Ouch! Tilly had just elbowed Adelle in the ribs.

"Avignon's last Pope left in 140 AD, but the Church still owned Avignon until the French Revolution in 1791."

Throughout their trip, various guides had referred to the French social uprising that began in 1787 and ended in 1799. The commoners had declared themselves a "National Assembly" able to write a new constitution, thus redefining the nature of political power. The Revolution put an end to the French monarchy, feudalism, and the political power of the Catholic church. In 1804, Napoleon Bonaparte, a general in the French army, seized power and crowned himself emperor. The palace was subsequently taken over by the Napoleonic French state for use as military barracks and a prison.

Another site repurposed.

Adelle thought of all the historic sites that had found new purposes in a new world. It dawned on her that she could do the same thing. Adelle smiled. She wasn't useless after all. She still had lots to offer.

"Although the palace was further damaged by the

military occupation, especially when the structure was eventually used as a stable, at least the shell of the building survived. It was vacated in 1906 when it became a national museum."

Repurposed again.

"The palace has been under constant restoration ever since," their guide said. "In my time, this site has been used for many cultural and economic events including exhibitions, shows, and conventions."

And tours.

Their guide presented their admission tickets at the entrance, and they proceeded into the palace. Since October of 2017, the entrance ticket price included the use of Histopads, augmented reality tablets that allowed users to see what the palace looked like over eight hundred years ago and how it had evolved. The colorful tablets brought many of the twenty-five rooms to life. All Adelle had to do was point the tablet at a room or artifact, and the screen would show her what it would have looked like all those years ago. Adelle felt like she was living in the Middle Ages.

Who knew using technology could be so much fun!

Evelyn was impressed by the papal apartments and their priceless frescoes painted by the Italian artist Matteo di Giovannetti. Debbie kept saying his name over and over until Tilly gave her the "shush" signal.

"It's fun to say," Debbie said, teasing her sister. "Matteo di Giovannetti, Matteo di Giovannetti."

Adelle used her Histopad and studied the informative plaques, models, illustrations, and reproductions. In the large dining room, which had the capacity for five hundred to seven hundred people, depending on the seating requirements, she imagined one lavish banquet after another.

Before she knew it, Adelle found herself at the end of the palace tour.

Arriving at the gift shop at the back of the palace, she saw the ship's program director pointing at Barb in the wine section.

"Well?" Adelle asked, getting right to the point. "Did you find the missing funds?"

"Affirmative." Barb grinned from ear to ear.

As the tour reconvened outside, Barb told Adelle, Evelyn, Debbie, and Tilly that Teresa had confronted the accountant. He confessed to everything and handed over the passwords to the various holding company accounts. Most of the missing funds had been recovered.

Evelyn caught up to Adelle as their group followed the guide up to the park on top of the rocky ridge overlooking Avignon and the Rhône below. "Thank you, Adelle. My daughter looks so happy."

The two friends chuckled, listening as Tilly and Debbie told Barb about the palace tour. Debbie, arms flailing, described what people had worn during the Middle Ages while Tilly reported all the historical details.

"Barb told me that you helped her on the first trip," Evelyn said. "She received a promotion when she got home."

"That's great!" Adelle exclaimed. Barb worked so

hard. Adelle was genuinely pleased that Barb had been promoted.

Maybe that's why Barb wanted to solve the mystery herself this time.

Adelle smiled, thinking of her granddaughter when she was a toddler. Her favorite expression was "I do it."

The park was a delightful oasis of green space, fountains, benches under shady trees, and children feeding ducks and swans in a large pond. The highest point offered sweeping views of Avignon and the river valley.

Their guide pointed out the four arches of the Pont Saint-Bénézet jutting partway across the Rhône below. Originally, there had been twenty-two arches. Debbie started whistling.

I know that tune.

It was the famous children's ditty, "Sur le Pont d'Avignon," a French song that Adelle had learned in school, about dancing on the bridge of Avignon.

"Thanks, Sis," Tilly groaned. "That will keep playing in my head all day."

Adelle gazed down at the famous medieval bridge. Its construction and location were believed to have been inspired by a shepherd's religious vision. In the Middle Ages, the bridge was part of the most important pilgrimage routes between Spain and Italy. The structure was abandoned in the middle of the seventeenth century because the arches kept collapsing each time the Rhône flooded. It would be generations before another bridge would close the gap across the Rhône near Avignon.

Adelle looked around the ship's deck and smiled contentedly. Tilly and Mickey were comparing longevity notes. Earlier, Adelle had thanked Mickey for bringing attention to her self-defeating thinking. Mickey had laughed when Adelle had blurted "I love to travel, but no more guilt trips!"

Debbie was talking to the painter who was trying to keep her sketch pad safe from Debbie, talking with her hands as usual.

Barb and Evelyn were laughing at something on Barb's phone.

Adelle was curious. "What are you looking at?"

"Debbie's post of us dancing on the Avignon bridge," Evelyn replied, eyes twinkling.

It had been Adelle's idea. Barb's phone provided the music, and their Avignon tour guide had been happy to video them.

"Tilly thinks we dance like old geezers," Barb said.

Breathe Adelle, breathe. "Old geezers?"

Barb grinned. "Tilly taught me that expression when we said goodbye after our first trip. If anyone wanted to know what I had been working on, Tilly said to tell them that I was simply hanging out with old geezers."

Evelyn looked at Adelle. Adelle looked at Evelyn. They both burst out laughing at the same time.

When Debbie and Tilly joined them to see what was so funny, Barb disappeared for several minutes. She returned with wine glasses and two open bottles of

Châteauneuf du Pape. After pouring the wine, Barb stood to make a toast.

"On behalf of Teresa, thank you for helping us find her missing funds."

Debbie made a show of twirling her glass, then sniffed it appreciatively. "I smell berries."

"I taste raspberry and currants," Adelle added, proud of her memory.

"With a touch of thyme, clove, and vanilla," Evelyn chimed in.

Tilly chuckled and raised her glass higher. "And a hint of Jean-Luc!"

After some good-natured teasing, Adelle proposed her own toast. "To Barb, whose brilliant technology skills saved the day."

Barb grinned. "With a little help from my friends." She turned to Evelyn. "It's time to tell you how I got my promotion on our first trip."

As Barb filled Evelyn in on what had happened on their river cruise from Budapest to Amsterdam, Tilly leaned toward Adelle. "We've been talking about another river cruise together."

Debbie's eyes were dancing. "Have you seen everything you wanted to see in Paris?"

"Have you heard of the home of champagne?" Tilly asked. "Champagne is good for your heart, you know."

"Have you been to the Swiss Alps?" Debbie asked.

Adelle tingled with excitement.

"Not yet!"

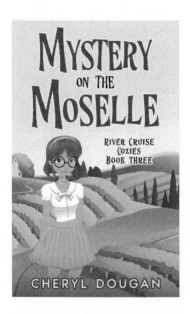

Hop Aboard *Mystery on the Moselle: River Cruise Cozies Book Three!*

Adelle is excited to get away on another river cruise with her girlfriends. But when her old friends accuse her new friends of theft, can she navigate the truth before all their careers sink?

Can Adelle solve the mystery and save everyone's reputation from sinking?

Read a sample of the first chapter of the next book for free!

Enter this address to get it delivered to your email!

https://tinyurl.com/cheryldougan3

GOOD KARMA

Thank you for reading *Passageways and Provence!*

Please take a moment to review this book. Your honest review will help future readers decide if they want to take a chance on a new-to-them author! An honest review is the greatest gift you can give an author.

You can go to the book directly on Amazon and leave a review!

If interested, please follow my author page on Amazon to learn about new releases! https://www.amazon.com/author/cheryldougan

ALSO BY CHERYL DOUGAN
RIVER CRUISE COZIES

A River Cruise Travel Mystery Series

Available on Amazon and Kindle Unlimited

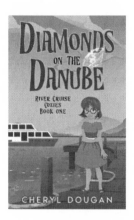

She gladly came out of retirement. She never expected to be cruising down the Danube trying to catch a diamond thief red-handed.

If you like globe-trotting heroines, quirky casts, and spectacular settings, then you'll love Cheryl Dougan's glittering whodunit.

She is excited to river cruise with her girlfriends again. But when one of them goes missing, can she solve the mystery before life goes overboard?

Will Adelle unravel all the mysteries in time to rescue her friends and regain their trust?

If you like armchair travel and heartwarming stories of friendship, you'll love Cheryl Dougan's sparkling new tale of intrigue.

Adelle is excited to get away on another river cruise with her girlfriends. But when her old friends accuse her new friends of theft, can she navigate the truth before all their careers sink?

Can Adelle solve the mystery and save everyone's reputation from sinking?

If you like unique characters, disentangling mysteries, and armchair travel in European settings, then you'll love Cheryl Dougan's newest tale of navigating friendships and intrigue.

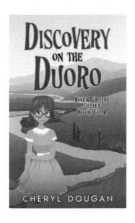

She expected to relax on her river cruise through Portugal. She didn't expect threats from the mafia.

Will Adelle discover the missing port before her new career sinks?

ABOUT THE AUTHOR

Cheryl has always loved reading and travelling. Recently she discovered her passion for writing travel cozy mysteries. When she is not reading, writing, or planning her next trip, she enjoys being outdoors, listening to her characters as they get excited about their next escapade.

Cheryl is the author of *Diamonds on the Danube*, *Passageways and Provence*, *Mystery on the Moselle*, and *Discovery on the Duoro*.

While she makes her home in Saskatchewan, Canada she is always on the lookout for her next adventure!

Find Cheryl online at: **www.cheryldouganauthor.com**

Manufactured by Amazon.ca
Bolton, ON

28606766R00069